A CHEST OF STORIES
FOR NINE YEAR OLDS

A CHEST

of Stories for Nine Year Olds

COLLECTED BY PAT THOMSON

Illustrated by Peter Bailey

CORGI BOOKS

A CHEST OF STORIES FOR NINE YEAR OLDS
A CORGI BOOK 0 552 527580

First published in Great Britain by Doubleday, a division of Transworld
Publishers Ltd.

PRINTING HISTORY
Doubleday edition published 1991
Corgi edition published 1992
Corgi edition reprinted 1993

Corgi Books are published by Transworld Publishers Ltd, 61–63
Uxbridge Road, Ealing, London W5 5SA, in Australia by Transworld
Publishers (Australia) Pty. Ltd, 15–25 Helles Avenue, Moorebank, NSW
2170, and in New Zealand by Transworld Publishers (N.Z.) Ltd,
3 William Pickering Drive, Albany, Auckland.

Printed and bound in Great Britain by Cox & Wyman Ltd,
Reading, Berks.

Acknowledgements

The editor and publisher are grateful for permission to include the following copyright material in this anthology.

Joan Aiken, 'The Cat Who Lived in a Drainpipe' from *The Faithless Lollybird and Other Stories*, text © 1977 by Joan Aiken Enterprises Ltd. Reprinted by permission of A M Heath & Company Ltd.

Mark Cohen, 'The Cat and the Dog' from *Don't Count Your Chickens & Other Fabulous Fables* by Mark Cohen (Viking Kestrel, 1989), © Mark Cohen 1989. Reprinted by permission of Penguin Books Ltd.

Richmal Crompton, 'William's Double Life', Chapter 3 from *William*. Reprinted by permission of Macmillan, London & Basingstoke and Mrs Richmal Crompton.

Peter Dickinson, 'Stone' from *Merlin Dreams*, text © Peter Dickinson 1988. Reprinted by permission of Victor Gollancz Ltd.

Nicholas Fisk, 'Sweets from a Stranger', © 1978 Nicholas Fisk. Reprinted by permission of Laura Cecil, Literary Agent for Children's Books.

Gene Kemp, 'Poor Arthur' from *Dog Days and Cat Naps* by Gene Kemp. Reprinted by permission of Faber and Faber Ltd.

Naomi Lewis, 'The Prince and the Tortoise' from *Stories From the Arabian Nights*, retold by Naomi Lewis, text © Naomi Lewis 1987. Reprinted by permission of Methuen Children's Books.

Margaret Mahy, 'The Hookywalker Dancers' from *The Door in the Air*, © Margaret Mahy 1988. Reprinted by permission of J M Dent & Sons Ltd, Publishers.

Jan Mark, from 'Nothing to Be Afraid Of' (Kestrel Books 1980), © Jan Mark 1980. Reprinted by permission of Penguin Books Ltd.

Philippa Pearce, 'The Shadow-Cage' from *The Shadow Cage and Other Tales* (Kestrel Books, 1977), © Philippa Pearce, 1977. Reprinted by permission of Penguin Books Ltd.

Susan Price, 'Lost Vanya' from *Here Lies Price*. Reprinted by permission of Faber and Faber Ltd.

Arthur Ransome, 'Baba Yaga' from *Old Peter's Russian Tales*. Reprinted by permission of the Estate of Arthur Ransome and Jonathan Cape as publishers.

Dinah Starkey, 'Lucott the Pirate' from *Ghosts and Bogles*, (William Heinemann Ltd.) © Dinah Starkey 1978. Reprinted by permission of the Octopus Publishing Group Library.

CONTENTS

Little Red Riding Hood: the Wolf's Story
by David Henry Wilson 1

The Shadow-Cage
by Philippa Pearce 11

Poor Arthur
by Gene Kemp 37

The Cat who Lived in a Drainpipe
by Joan Aiken 45

The Asrai
by Pat Thomson 89

The Cat and the Dog
by the Brothers Grimm, retold by Mark Cohen 95

The Prince and the Tortoise
*a retelling by Naomi Lewis of the traditional
Arabian Nights tale* 103

Nothing to be Afraid of
by Jan Mark 115

Lucott the Pirate
by Dinah Starkey 127

Stone
by Peter Dickinson 139

Baba Yaga
*a retelling by Arthur Ransome of the Russian
fairy tale*   153

Sweets from a Stranger
by Nicholas Fisk   169

Lost Vanya
by Susan Price   187

William's Double Life
by Richmal Crompton   197

The Hookywalker Dancers
by Margaret Mahy   227

A CHEST OF STORIES
FOR NINE YEAR OLDS

Little Red Riding Hood:
the Wolf's Story

OK, so I got killed in the end and you all said yippee. I'm not complaining about that. I wasn't as clever as I thought I was, so I'll take my defeat like a wolf. But now that I'm a was-wolf (that is, a dead wolf), and I'm up here in Valhowla (paradise for wolves), I'll rest a lot easier if the record is set straight. The official accounts of what happened that day are all lies, and I hate lies – especially lies about me. So here's the story of what really happened.

The first lie that annoys me is all this big-bad-wolf business. Big? I may have been average size once, but by the time I was killed, I was more ribs than muscles. I hadn't had a decent meal in weeks. Skinny, yes – big, no. And why bad? What was ever bad about me? I reckon I'm one of the nicest wolves I know. So instead of, *In the forest there lived a big bad wolf*, now read, *In the forest there lived a skinny nice wolf*.

Next we come to the question of motive. The history books say I wanted to eat Little Red Riding Hood. I didn't, and I can prove it. But even if I *had* wanted to eat her, what's so terrible about that? When she had eggs and bacon for breakfast, did anyone complain that big bad Red Riding Hood took the eggs from the chicken as well as two slices off Porky Pig? When she had roast turkey for Christmas, did it bother her what might have happened to Mrs Turkey and all the little Turks? When she sank her teeth into a juicy rump steak, did she spare a thought for some poor cow walking round the field with half its bottom missing? What's the difference between a little girl eating me and my mates, and me eating a little girl?

Anyway, as I said, I didn't want to eat her. Here's the proof. You remember she and I had a little chat in the woods? I asked her where she was going, what she had in the basket, and where her sick granny lived. Well, if I was close enough to talk to her, you'll have to agree that I was close enough to eat her. Why didn't I? Some of the accounts suggest it was because there were some woodcutters nearby. Rubbish. If there'd been a single woodcutter nearby, I'd have been off faster than you can say, 'The wonderful wolf went away from the wood.'

The fact is, I was after Red Riding Hood's basket with all the goodies in it. With my blunt old teeth I couldn't even bite a chicken, let alone a little girl. It was the basket I wanted. I thought of stealing it from her there and then, but for three reasons I didn't. First, I didn't want to upset her. Second, she might have started screaming, and I don't like screams, or people who hear screams. And third, she might not have let go, and I was in no condition for a fight.

My plan was very simple. I intended to pop along to Granny's cottage, give her a little scare so she'd run away for a few minutes, pretend I was Granny, and relieve Red Riding Hood of the basket. Then she would have gone home thinking she'd done her good deed, Granny would have come back feeling pleased she'd escaped from the wolf, and I'd have got the basket. We'd all have lived happily ever after.

Only things didn't quite work out that way. First of all, in spite of what the official reports might say, Granny wasn't there. I pushed open the door, all set to say 'boo' and get out of the way as she rushed out, but there was nobody to say 'boo' to. Actually, I was rather glad, because some grannies don't scare easily. I've seen grannies that scared me a good deal more than I scared them. Anyway, the room was empty, so I reckoned it was my lucky day. I crawled into bed, pulling the covers over me.

In a few minutes, Little Red Riding Hood came along, and again the history books have got it all wrong. Unless she was as short-sighted as a one-eyed rhinoceros, do you honestly think she would have taken me for her grandmother? All those lies about 'what big teeth you have', and so on. I'll tell you exactly what we said to each other.

When she knocked at the door, I stayed under the covers and called out: 'Who is it?' (That was rather clever of me. I knew who it was, but Granny wouldn't have known, would she?)

'It's me, Grandma!' said Red Riding Hood.

'Who's me?' I asked.

'You's you!' she replied.

had put three bullets right where I should have had the fruit cake and chocolate biscuits. I collapsed like a chopped tree.

'Good shooting, Grandma!' said Red Riding Hood – though what was good about it I shall never know.

'Quick, fetch the vet!' I gasped.

But the last thing those two had in mind was to help poor dying Wolfie.

'We ought to get the newspapers here,' said Granny. 'This could be quite a story.'

'Oh, yes,' said Red Riding Hood. 'They might publish our pictures and we'd be famous!'

And while I lay there, half in and half out of the world, they calmly discussed the tale they would tell the reporters. Granny was worried that she might get into trouble because she didn't have a licence for her gun. (I wish she'd thought of that earlier.) Red Riding Hood also wondered why Granny hadn't been in her bed, because she was supposed to be sick. It turned out that Granny had been on the lavatory, but she certainly wasn't going to tell *that* to the reporters.

'And what,' said Granny, 'are they going to think when they find the wolf in my bed? After all, I've got my reputation to think of.'

'Blow your reputation,' I groaned. 'What about me? I've been shot!'

'You keep out of this, Wolfie,' said Granny.

'You've caused enough trouble as it is.'

I'd caused trouble! Was it my fault she'd been on the lavatory? And who fired the gun? And who didn't have a licence? But it was no use arguing – they'd made up their minds that I was the villain and they were the heroes.

'Perhaps,' said Red Riding Hood, 'we can pretend someone else shot him – a hunter, or a woodcutter.'

'But that wouldn't explain how he got into my bed,' said Granny.

'I know what,' cried Red Riding Hood. 'We could say you were in bed, and Wolfie came in and ate you.'

'You must be joking,' I moaned. 'With my teeth I couldn't even eat a chicken, let alone a tough old bird like Granny.'

'Keep quiet, Wolfie!' said Granny. 'No, the problem there, my dear, is that if he'd eaten me, I'd be dead. And I'm not.'

'Well,' said Red Riding Hood, 'we could say he ate you whole, and then the woodcutter cut him open and you came out alive.'

'Now that's an idea!' said Granny.

'Oh, yeah!' I gasped. 'A newborn fifteen-stone sixty-year-old baby! Who's going to believe that?'

'Then,' continued the Little Red Liar, 'we'll say he disguised himself as you, I came in, and the woodcutter rescued me in the nick of time.'

'Oh, well,' I groaned, 'why don't I eat a whole

Red Riding Hood for dessert – make a proper meal of it?'

'Why not?' asked Granny.

'You're both crazy!' I panted. 'Nobody in this whole wide world can be stupid enough to swallow a story like that!'

Those were my last words. With one more bullet from Granny, I huffed my last puff. But I died happy in the knowledge that nobody in the whole wide world could be stupid enough to swallow a story like that. Ugh, how wrong can a wolf be?

This story is by David Henry Wilson.

The Shadow-Cage

The little green stoppered bottle had been waiting in the earth a long time for someone to find it. Ned Challis found it. High on his tractor as he ploughed the field, he'd been keeping a look-out, as usual, for whatever might turn up. Several times there had been worked flints; once, one of an enormous size.

Now sunlight glimmering on glass caught his eye. He stopped the tractor, climbed down, picked the bottle from the earth. He could tell at once that it wasn't all that old. Not as old as the flints that he'd taken to the museum in Castleford. Not as old as a coin he had once found, with the head of a Roman emperor on it. Not very old; but old.

Perhaps just useless old . . .

He held the bottle in the palm of his hand and thought of throwing it away. The lip of it was chipped badly, and the stopper of cork or wood had sunk into the neck. With his fingernail he tried to move it. The stopper had hardened into stone, and stuck there. Probably no-one would ever get it out now without breaking the bottle. But then, why should anyone want to unstopper the bottle? It was empty, or as good as empty. The bottom of the inside of the bottle was dirtied with something blackish and scaly that also clung a little to the sides.

He wanted to throw the bottle away, but he didn't. He held it in one hand while the fingers of the other cleaned the remaining earth from the outside. When he had cleaned it, he didn't fancy the bottle any more than before; but he dropped it into his pocket. Then he climbed the tractor and started off again.

At that time the sun was high in the sky, and the tractor was working on Whistlers' Hill, which is part of Belper's Farm, fifty yards below Burnt House. As the tractor moved on again, the gulls followed again, rising and falling in their flights, wheeling over the disturbed earth, looking for live things, for food; for good things.

That evening, at tea, Ned Challis brought the bottle out and set it on the table by the loaf of bread. His wife looked at it suspiciously: 'Another of your dirty old things for that museum?'

Ned said: 'It's not museum-stuff. Lisa can have it to take to school. I don't want it.'

Mrs Challis pursed her lips, moved the loaf

further away from the bottle, and went to refill the tea-pot.

Lisa took the bottle in her hand. 'Where'd you get it, Dad?'

'Whistlers' Hill. Just below Burnt House.' He frowned suddenly as he spoke, as if he had remembered something.

'What's it got inside?'

'Nothing. And if you try getting the stopper out, that'll break.'

So Lisa didn't try. Next morning she took it to school; but she didn't show it to anyone. Only her cousin Kevin saw it, and that was before school and by accident. He always called for Lisa on his way to school – there was no other company on that country road – and he saw her pick up the bottle from the table, where her mother had left it the night before, and put it into her anorak pocket.

'What was that?' asked Kevin.

'You saw. A little old bottle.'

'Let's see it again – properly.' Kevin was younger than Lisa, and she sometimes indulged him; so she took the bottle out and let him hold it.

At once he tried the stopper.

'Don't,' said Lisa. 'You'll only break it.'

'What's inside?'

'Nothing. Dad found it on Whistlers'.'

'It's not very nice, is it?'

'What do you mean, "Not very nice"?'

'I don't know. But let me keep it for a bit. Please, Lisa.'

On principle Lisa now decided not to give in. 'Certainly not. Give it back.'

He did, reluctantly. 'Let me have it just for today, at school. Please.'

'No.'

'I'll give you something if you'll let me have it. I'll not let anyone else touch it; I'll not let them see it. I'll keep it safe. Just for today.'

'You'd only break it. No. What could you give me, anyway?'

14

'My week's pocket-money.'

'No. I've said no and I mean no, young Kev.'

'I'd give you that little china dog you like.'

'The one with the china kennel?'

'Yes.'

'The china dog with the china kennel – you'd give me both?'

'Yes.'

'Only for half the day, then,' said Lisa. 'I'll let you have it after school-dinner – look out for me in the playground. Give it back at the end of school. Without fail. And you be careful with it.'

So the bottle travelled to school in Lisa's anorak pocket, where it bided its time all morning. After school-dinner Lisa met Kevin in the playground and they withdrew together to a corner which was well away from the crowded climbing-frame and the infants' sandpit and the rest. Lisa handed the bottle over. 'At the end of school, mind, without fail. And if we miss each other then,' – for Lisa, being in a higher class, came out of school slightly later than Kevin – 'then you must drop it in at ours as you pass. Promise.'

'Promise.'

They parted. Kevin put the bottle into his pocket. He didn't know why he'd wanted the bottle, but he had. Lots of things were like that. You needed them for a bit; and then you didn't need them any longer.

He had needed this little bottle very much.

He left Lisa and went over to the climbing-frame, where his friends already were. He had set his foot on a rung when he thought suddenly how easy it would be for the glass bottle in his trouser pocket to be smashed against the metal framework. He stepped down again and went over to the fence that separated the playground from the farmland beyond. Tall tussocks of grass grew along it, coming through from the open fields and fringing the very edge of the asphalt. He looked round: Lisa had already gone in, and no-one else was watching. He put his hand into his pocket and took it out again with the bottle concealed in the fist. He stooped as if to examine an insect on a tussock, and slipped his hand into the middle of it and left the bottle there, well hidden.

He straightened up and glanced around. Since no-one was looking in his direction, his action had been unobserved; the bottle would be safe. He ran back to the climbing-frame and began to climb, jostling and shouting and laughing, as he and his friends always did. He forgot the bottle.

He forgot the bottle completely.

It was very odd, considering what a fuss he had made about the bottle, that he should have forgotten it; but he did. When the bell rang for the end of playtime, he ran straight in. He did not think of the bottle then, or later. At the end of afternoon school, he did not remember it; and he happened not to see Lisa, who would surely have reminded him.

Only when he was nearly home, and passing the Challises' house, he remembered. He had faithfully promised – and had really meant to keep his promise. But he'd broken it, and left the bottle behind. If he turned and went back to school now, he would meet Lisa, and she would have to be told . . . By the time he got back to the school playground, all his friends would have gone home: the caretaker would be there, and perhaps a late teacher or two, and they'd all want to know what he was up to. And when he'd got the bottle and dropped it in at the Challises', Lisa would scold him all over again. And when he got home at last, he would be very late for his tea, and his mother would be angry.

As he stood by the Challises' gate, thinking, it seemed best, since he had messed things up anyway, to go straight home and leave the bottle to the next day. So he went home.

He worried about the bottle for the rest of the day, without having the time or the quiet to think about it very clearly. He knew that Lisa would assume he had just forgotten to leave it at her house on the way home. He half expected her to turn up after tea, to claim it; but she didn't. She would have been angry enough about his having forgotten to leave it; but what about her anger tomorrow on the way to school, when she found that he had forgotten it altogether – abandoned it in the open playground? He thought of hurrying straight past her house in the morning; but he would never manage it. She would be on the look-out.

He saw that he had made the wrong decision earlier. He ought, at all costs, to have gone back to the playground to get the bottle.

He went to bed, still worrying. He fell asleep, and his worry went on, making his dreaming unpleasant in a nagging way. He must be quick, his dreams seemed to nag. *Be quick* . . .

Suddenly he was wide awake. It was very late. The sound of the television being switched off must have woken him. Quietness. He listened to the rest of the family going to bed. They went to bed and to sleep. Silence. They were all asleep now, except for him. He couldn't sleep.

Then, as abruptly as if someone had lifted the top of his head like a lid and popped the idea in, he saw that this time – almost the middle of the night – was the perfect time for him to fetch the bottle. He knew by heart the roads between home and school; he would not be afraid. He would have plenty of time. When he reached the school, the gate to the playground would be shut, but it was not high: in the past, by daylight, he and his friends had often climbed it. He would go into the playground, find the correct tussock of grass, get the bottle, bring it back, and have it ready to give to Lisa on the way to school in the morning. She would be angry, but only moderately angry. She would never know the whole truth.

He got up and dressed quickly and quietly. He began to look for a pocket-torch, but gave up when he realized that would mean opening and shutting drawers and cupboards. Anyway, there was a moon tonight, and he knew his way, and he knew the school playground. He couldn't go wrong.

He let himself out of the house, leaving the door on the latch for his return. He looked at his watch: between a quarter and half past eleven – not as late as he had thought. All the same, he set off almost at a run, but had to settle down into a steady trot. His trotting footsteps on the road sounded clearly in the night quiet. But who was there to hear?

He neared the Challises' house. He drew level with it.

Ned Challis heard. Usually nothing woke him before the alarm-clock in the morning, but tonight footsteps woke him. Who, at this hour – he lifted the back of his wrist towards his face, so that the time glimmered at him – who, at nearly twenty-five to twelve, could be hurrying along that road on foot? When the footsteps had almost gone – when it was already perhaps too late he sprang

19

out of bed and over to the window.

His wife woke. 'What's up, then, Ned?'

'Just somebody. I wondered who.'

'Oh, come back to bed!'

Ned Challis went back to bed; but almost at once got out again.

'Ned! What is it now?'

'I just thought I'd have a look at Lisa.'

At once Mrs Challis was wide awake. 'What's wrong with Lisa?'

'Nothing.' He went to listen at Lisa's door – listen to the regular, healthy breathing of her sleep. He came back. 'Nothing. Lisa's all right.'

'For heaven's sake! Why shouldn't she be?'

'Well, who was it walking out there? Hurrying.'

'Oh, go to sleep!'

'Yes.' He lay down again, drew the bedclothes round him, lay still. But his eyes remained open.

Out in the night, Kevin left the road on which the Challises lived and came into the more important one that would take him into the village. He heard the rumble of a lorry coming up behind him. For safety he drew right into a gateway and waited. The lorry came past at a steady pace, headlights on. For a few seconds he saw the driver and his mate sitting up in the cab, intent on the road ahead. He had not wanted to be noticed by them, but, when they had gone, he felt lonely.

He went on into the village, its houses

lightless, its streets deserted. By the entrance to the school driveway, he stopped to make sure he was unobserved. Nobody. Nothing – not even a cat. There was no sound of any vehicle now; but in the distance he heard a dog barking, and then another answered it. A little owl cried and cried for company or for sport. Then that, too, stopped.

He turned into the driveway to the school, and there was the gate to the playground. He looked over it, into the playground. Moonlight showed him everything: the expanse of asphalt, the sand-pit, the big climbing-frame, and – at the far end – the fence with the tussocks of grass growing blackly along it. It was all familiar, and yet strange because of the emptiness and the whitening of moonlight and the shadows cast like solid things. The climbing-frame reared high into the air, and on the ground stretched the black criss-cross of its shadows like the bars of a cage.

But he had not come all this way to be halted by moonshine and insubstantial shadows. In a businesslike way he climbed the gate and crossed the playground to the fence. He wondered whether he would find the right tussock easily, but he did. His fingers closed on the bottle: it was waiting for him.

At that moment, in the Challises' house, as they lay side by side in bed, Mrs Challis said to her husband: 'You're still awake, aren't you?'

'Yes.'

'What is it?'

'Nothing.'

Mrs Challis sighed.

'All right, then,' said Ned Challis. 'It's this. That bottle I gave Lisa – that little old bottle that I gave Lisa yesterday —'

'What about it?'

'I found it by Burnt House.'

Mrs Challis drew in her breath sharply. Then she said, 'That may mean nothing.' Then, 'How near was it?'

'Near enough.' After a pause: 'I ought never to have given it to Lisa. I never thought. But Lisa's all right, anyway.'

'But, Ned, don't you know what Lisa did with that bottle?'

'What?'

'Lent it to Kevin to have at school. And, according to her, he didn't return it when he should have done, on the way home. Didn't you hear her going on and on about it?'

'Kevin . . .' For the third time that night Ned Challis was getting out of bed, this time putting on his trousers, fumbling for his shoes. 'Somebody went up the road in a hurry. You know – I looked out. I couldn't see properly, but it was somebody small. It could have been a child. It could have been Lisa, but it wasn't. It could well have been Kevin . . .'

'Shouldn't you go to their house first, Ned – find out whether Kevin is there or not? Make sure. You're not sure.'

'I'm not sure. But, if I wait to make sure, I may be too late.'

Mrs Challis did not say, 'Too late for what?' She did not argue.

Ned Challis dressed and went down. As he let himself out of the house to get his bicycle from the shed, the church clock began to strike the hour, the sound reaching him distantly across the intervening fields. He checked with his watch: midnight.

In the village, in the school playground, the striking of midnight sounded clangorously close. Kevin stood with the bottle held in the palm of his hand, waiting for the clock to stop striking – waiting as if for something to follow.

After the last stroke of midnight, there was silence, but Kevin still stood waiting and listening. A car or lorry passed the entrance of the school drive: he heard it distinctly; yet it was oddly faint, too. He couldn't place the oddness of it. It had sounded much further away than it should have done – less really there.

He gripped the bottle and went on listening, as if for some particular sound. The minutes passed.

The same dog barked at the same dog, bark and reply – far, unreally far away. The little owl called; from another world, it might have been.

He was gripping the bottle so tightly now that his hand was sweating. He felt his skin begin to prickle with sweat at the back of his neck and under his arms.

Then there was a whistle from across the fields, distantly. It should have been an unexpected sound, just after midnight; but it did not startle him. It did set him off across the playground, however. Too late he wanted to get away. He had to go past the climbing-frame, whose cagework of shadows now stretched more largely than the frame itself. He saw the bars of shadow as he approached; he actually hesitated; and then, like a fool, he stepped inside the cage of shadows.

Ned Challis, on his bicycle, had reached the junction of the by-road with the road that – in one direction – led to the village. In the other it led deeper into the country. Which way? He dismounted. He had to choose the right way – to follow Kevin.

Thinking of Whistlers' Hill, he turned the front wheel of his bicycle away from the village and set off again. But now, with his back to the village, going away from the village, he felt a kind of weariness and despair. A memory of childhood came into his mind: a game he had played in childhood: something hidden for him to find, and if he turned in the wrong direction to search, all the voices whispered to him, 'Cold – cold!' Now, with the village receding behind him, he recognized what he felt: cold . . . cold . . .

Without getting off his bicycle, he wheeled round and began to pedal hard in the direction of the village.

In the playground, there was no pressing hurry for Kevin any more. He did not press against the bars of his cage to get out. Even when clouds cut off the moonlight and the shadows melted into general darkness – even when the shadow-cage was no longer visible to the eye, he stood there; then crouched there, in a corner of the cage, as befitted a prisoner.

The church clock struck the quarter.

The whistlers were in no hurry. The first whistle had come from right across the fields. Then there was a long pause. Then the sound was repeated, equally distantly, from the direction of the river bridges. Later still, another whistle from the direction of the railway line, or somewhere near it.

He lay in his cage, cramped by the bars, listening. He did not know he was thinking, but suddenly it came to him: Whistlers' Hill. He and Lisa and the others had always supposed that the hill had belonged to a family called Whistler, as Challises' house belonged to the Challis family. But that was not how the hill had got its name – he saw that now. No, indeed not.

Whistler answered whistler at long intervals, like the sentries of a besieging army. There was no moving in as yet.

The church clock had struck the quarter as Ned Challis entered the village and cycled past the entrance to the school. He cycled as far as the Recreation Ground, perhaps because that was where Kevin would have gone in the daytime. He cycled bumpily round the Ground: no Kevin.

He began to cycle back the way he had come, as though he had given up altogether and was going home. He cycled slowly. He passed the entrance to the school again.

In this direction, he was leaving the village.

26

He was cycling so slowly that the front wheel of his bicycle wobbled desperately; the light from his dynamo was dim. He put a foot down and stopped. Motionless, he listened. There was nothing to hear, unless – yes, the faintest ghost of a sound, high pitched, prolonged for seconds, remote as from another world. Like a coward – and Ned Challis was no coward – he tried to persuade himself he had imagined the sound; yet he knew he had not. It came from another direction now: very faint, yet penetrating, so that his skin crinkled to hear it. Again it came, from yet another quarter.

He wheeled his bicycle back to the entrance to the school and left it there. He knew he must be very close. He walked up to the playground gate and peered over it. But the moon was obscured by cloud: he could see nothing. He listened, waiting for the moon to sail free.

In the playground Kevin had managed to get up, first on his hands and knees, then upright. He was very much afraid, but he had to be standing to meet whatever it was.

For the whistlers had begun to close in slowly, surely: converging on the school, on the school playground, on the cage of shadows. On him.

For some time now cloud-masses had obscured the moon. He could see nothing; but he felt the whistlers' presence. Their signals came more often, and always closer. Closer. Very close.

Suddenly the moon sailed free.

In the sudden moonlight Ned Challis saw clear across the playground to where Kevin stood against the climbing-frame, with his hands writhing together in front of him.

In the sudden moonlight Kevin did not see his uncle. Between him and the playground gate, and all around him, air was thickening into darkness. Frantically he tried to undo his fingers, that held the little bottle, so that he could throw it from him. But he could not. He held the bottle; the bottle held him.

The darkness was closing in on him. The darkness was about to take him; had surely got him.

Kevin shrieked.

Ned Challis shouted: 'I'm here!' and was over the gate and across the playground and with his arms round the boy: '*I've got you.*'

There was a tinkle as something fell from between Kevin's opened fingers: the little bottle fell and rolled to the middle of the playground. It lay there, very insignificant-looking.

Kevin was whimpering and shaking, but he could move of his own accord. Ned Challis helped him over the gate and to the bicycle.

'Do you think you could sit on the bar, Kev? Could you manage that?'

'Yes.' He could barely speak.

Ned Challis hesitated, thinking of the bottle

which had chosen to come to rest in the very centre of the playground, where the first child tomorrow would see it, pick it up.

He went back and picked the bottle up. Wherever he threw it, someone might find it. He might smash it and grind the pieces underfoot; but he was not sure he dared to do that.

Anyway, he was not going to hold it in his hand longer than he strictly must. He put it into his pocket, and then, when he got back to Kevin and the bicycle, he slipped it into the saddle-bag.

He rode Kevin home on the cross-bar of his bicycle. At the Challises' front gate Mrs Challis was waiting, with the dog for company. She just said: 'He all right then?'

'Ah.'

'I'll make a cup of tea while you take him home.'

At his own front door, Kevin said: 'I left the door on the latch. I can get in. I'm all right. I'd rather – I'd rather —'

'Less spoken of, the better,' said his uncle. 'You go to bed. Nothing to be afraid of now.'

He waited until Kevin was inside the house and he heard the latch click into place. Then he rode back to his wife, his cup of tea, and consideration of the problem that lay in his saddle-bag.

After he had told his wife everything, and they had discussed possibilities, Ned Challis said thoughtfully: 'I might take it to the museum, after all. Safest place for it would be inside a glass case there.'

'But you said they wouldn't want it.'

'Perhaps they would, if I told them where I found it and a bit – only a bit – about Burnt House . . .'

'You do that, then.'

Ned Challis stood up and yawned with a finality that said, Bed.

'But don't you go thinking you've solved all your problems by taking that bottle to Castleford, Ned. Not by a long chalk.'

'No?'

'Lisa. She reckons she owns that bottle.'

'I'll deal with Lisa tomorrow.'

'Today, by the clock.'

Ned Challis gave a groan that turned into another yawn. 'Bed first,' he said; 'then Lisa.' They went to bed not long before the dawn.

The next day and for days after that, Lisa was furiously angry with her father. He had as good as stolen her bottle, she said, and now he refused to give it back, to let her see it, even to tell her what he had done with it. She was less angry with Kevin. (She did not know, of course, the circumstances of the bottle's passing from Kevin to her father.)

Kevin kept out of Lisa's way, and even more carefully kept out of his uncle's. He wanted no private conversation.

One Saturday Kevin was having tea at the

Challises', because he had been particularly invited. He sat with Lisa and Mrs Challis. Ned had gone to Castleford, and came in late. He joined them at the tea-table in evident good spirits. From his pocket he brought out a small cardboard box, which he placed in the centre of the table, by the Saturday cake. His wife was staring at him: before he spoke, he gave her the slightest nod of reassurance. 'The museum didn't want to keep that little old glass bottle, after all,' he said.

Both the children gave a cry: Kevin started up with such a violent backward movement that his chair clattered to the floor behind him; Lisa lent forward, her fingers clawing towards the box.

'No!' Ned Challis said. To Lisa he added: 'There it stays, girl, till *I* say.' To Kevin: 'Calm down. Sit up at the table again and listen to me.' Kevin picked his chair up and sat down again, resting his elbows on the table, so that his hands supported his head.

'Now,' said Ned Challis, 'you two know so much that it's probably better you should know more. That little old bottle came from Whistlers' Hill, below Burnt House – well, you know that. Burnt House is only a ruin now – elder bushes growing inside as well as out; but once it was a cottage that someone lived in. Your mother's granny remembered the last one to live there.'

'No, Ned,' said Mrs Challis, 'it was my great-granny remembered.'

'Anyway,' said Ned Challis, 'it was so long ago

that Victoria was the Queen, that's certain. And an old woman lived alone in that cottage. There were stories about her.'

'Was she a witch?' breathed Lisa.

'So they said. They said she went out on the hillside at night —'

'At the full of the moon,' said Mrs Challis.

'They said she dug up roots and searched out plants and toadstools and things. They said she caught rats and toads and even bats. They said she made ointments and powders and weird brews. And they said she used what she made to cast spells and call up spirits.'

'Spirits from Hell, my great-granny said. Real bad 'uns.'

'So people said, in the village. Only the parson scoffed at the whole idea. Said he'd called often and been shown over the cottage and seen nothing out of the ordinary – none of the jars and bottles of stuff that she was supposed to have for her witchcraft. He said she was just a poor cranky old woman; that was all.

'Well, she grew older and older and crankier and crankier, and one day she died. Her body lay in its coffin in the cottage, and the parson was going to bury her next day in the churchyard.

'The night before she was to have been buried, someone went up from the village —'

'Someone!' said Mrs Challis scornfully. 'Tell them the whole truth, Ned, if you're telling the story at all. Half the village went up, with lanterns – men, women, and children. Go on, Ned.'

'The cottage was thatched, and they began to pull swatches of straw away and take it into the cottage and strew it round and heap it up under the coffin. They were going to fire it all.

'They were pulling the straw on the downhill side of the cottage when suddenly a great piece of thatch came away and out came tumbling a whole lot of things that the old woman must have kept hidden there. People did hide things in thatches, in those days.'

'Her savings?' asked Lisa.

'No. A lot of jars and little bottles, all stoppered or sealed, neat and nice. With stuff inside.'

There was a silence at the tea-table. Then Lisa said: 'That proved it: she was a witch.'

'Well, no, it only proved she *thought* she was a witch. That was what the parson said afterwards – and whew! was he mad when he knew about that night.'

Mrs Challis said: 'He gave it 'em red hot from the pulpit the next Sunday. He said that once upon a time poor old deluded creatures like her had been burnt alive for no reason at all, and the village ought to be ashamed of having burnt her dead.'

Lisa went back to the story of the night itself. 'What did they do with what came out of the thatch?'

'Bundled it inside the cottage among the straw, and fired it all. The cottage burnt like a beacon that night, they say. Before cockcrow, everything had been burnt to ashes. That's the end of the story.'

'Except for my little bottle,' said Lisa. 'That came out of the thatch, but it didn't get picked up. It rolled downhill, or someone kicked it.'

'That's about it,' Ned agreed.

Lisa stretched her hand again to the cardboard box, and this time he did not prevent her. But he said: 'Don't be surprised, Lisa. It's different.'

She paused. 'A different bottle?'

'The same bottle, but – well, you'll see.'

Lisa opened the box, lifted the packaging of cotton wool, took the bottle out. It was the same bottle, but the stopper had gone, and it was empty and clean – so clean that it shone greenly. Innocence shone from it.

'You said the stopper would never come out,' Lisa said slowly.

'They forced it by suction. The museum chap wanted to know what was inside, so he got the hospital lab to take a look – he has a friend there. It was easy for them.'

Mrs Challis said: 'That would make a pretty vase, Lisa. For tiny flowers.' She coaxed Lisa to go out to pick a posy from the garden; she herself took the bottle away to fill it with water.

Ned Challis and Kevin faced each other across the table.

Kevin said: 'What was in it?'

Ned Challis said: 'A trace of this, a trace of that, the hospital said. One thing more than anything else.'

'Yes?'

'Blood. Human blood.'

Lisa came back with her flowers; Mrs Challis came back with the bottle filled with water. When the flowers had been put in, it looked a pretty thing.

'My witch-bottle,' said Lisa contentedly. 'What was she called – the old woman that thought she was a witch?'

Her father shook his head; her mother thought: 'Madge – or was it Maggy —?'

'Maggy Whistler's bottle, then,' said Lisa.

'Oh, no,' said Mrs Challis. 'She was Maggy – or Madge – Dawson. I remember my granny saying so. Dawson.'

'Then why's it called Whistlers' Hill?'

'I'm not sure,' said Mrs Challis uneasily. 'I mean, I don't think anyone knows for certain.'

But Ned Challis, looking at Kevin's face, knew that he knew for certain.

This story is by Philippa Pearce.

Poor Arthur

After Dennis, the cat, had caught the white mouse
one day when the cage was being cleaned out – by
Bloggs, my stupid sister, of course – I wouldn't
have let it happen, only she's so slow, she didn't
see Dennis coming like a streak of death across the
floor, up on to the table, and to where that white
mouse was just running round and round, then
Mum said there weren't to be any more animals,
because she couldn't stand the smell, and she was
the only one that fed them.

Well, we took to moaning about having no
animals except the cat, Dennis, you remember,
and he's so old I'm sure he was never a kitten, older
than me and always asleep except when he's hunting
defenceless birds and mice, and being all streaky and
murderous, and then we took to hanging around
petshops and looking at the creatures. I fancied a
yellow spotted snake and Bloggs a Great Dane,
but we didn't have much hopes of either, really,
not with our mum.

Then, just at the right moment, our next door neighbour said she'd got gerbils, and they were very nice, and you didn't have to clean them out often as they didn't smell.

'All animals smell,' said Mum.

The next door neighbour took us all round to the gerbillery, I suppose you could call it, as there were two couples and two sets of baby gerbils.

'I'll give you one for your birthday,' she said, as I stood there letting them run over me, with my inside swimming with joy at the feel of their fur and their little soft claws. And Mum said all right, then, providing you look after them, not me.

So we cleaned up the old mouse cage, then rushed off to buy sawdust and gerbil food.

And so came Chuchi.

Not that we called her Chuchi at first. We tried Polly, and Nosey, and Cleo, but nothing fitted. She wasn't much to look at, a bit tatty, really, with ruffled fur and a big hooked nose which she poked into everything. But she had bright black eyes and she ran to us whenever we came near, head cocked on one side, chattering furiously, hiding nuts, eating nuts, tearing up toilet rolls, kicking angrily with her back feet when she was in a temper. Dad called her the little rat. He was always chatting to her or tempting her with peanuts so that she'd jump really high. Even Mum took to her. She let me have her in my bedroom because the cage didn't smell, and at night I'd let her run round my bed and snuggle in my pyjama pocket.

And she still hadn't got a name.

Only one day Mum said, out of the blue, 'Let's go and get some grass seeds for Chuchi. She likes grass seeds.'

'Chuchi?'

'Yes, Chuchi, of course,' as if we ought to have known all along. 'That's the sound we make when we want her to come to us, and it's her funny chatter noise as well.'

So there she was. Chuchi. Named at last.

Now all this time we'd kept an eye on Dennis, that hunting cat. There was no smell to tempt him, but he knew something very interesting was going on. Dennis is a clever cat. Watches and waits. Sometimes we'd find him outside my room, washing himself very innocently. Chuchi grew bad-tempered. Straw and shredded toilet rolls flew through the air.

'She needs a mate,' Dad announced at tea-time.

'Babies,' Bloggs cried, stupid eyes shining.

'I like Chuchi, but enough is enough,' Mum said.

'Females need mating,' Dad said. 'That's why she's irritable. Females do get irritable.'

'Humph,' snorted Mum, banging down scrambled eggs on the table. I thought for a minute she was going to bang them on his head.

We bought another gerbil.

Dad built a second cage in case they didn't get on, and for the babies later.

This turned out to be a good thing, because Chuchi took a violent dislike to the new gerbil, and chased him out, biting and kicking like fury. He was terrified and squealed pitifully, poor little thing, only half her size. We called him Arthur. The next day we tried to put him in with her again, but it was no good. The cage was her territory and she wasn't having Arthur in it.

Then Dad thought of putting the cages together, and soon they were sniffing each other through the wire.

A week later they were both living happily in Chuchi's cage. Arthur grew bigger and braver but she was still the boss. They looked very alike now, though Chuchi still had the longer tail and the bigger nose, and a more untidy look.

Dennis the hunter waited, licking his tabby fur. Patient, wicked Dennis.

'I do wish she'd have babies,' sighed Bloggs.

'Well, she's getting fatter,' Mum said.

My dad drives a bus, and works different shifts. That day he'd gone to work very early, returned at ten in the morning, and gone out again at three. We came home with Mum, who's a teacher, at four. There was a note for us on the table. Dad in a temper is like Vesuvius erupting. The note said:

'If I find out who left the cage door open this morning, you'll wish you'd never been born, for that murdering cat has killed Chuchi. I've tried to catch him but he was too fast, which is just as well for him.'

He'd put her on the sideboard, and she was stiff and cold, but her fur was as soft as ever. Mum was sobbing, and tears were streaming down Bloggs's face. I didn't cry. I just stood there, stroking her over and over again.

'We must bury her,' Mum said, at last.

I found a Dinky car-container with a transparent top, and Bloggs put her inside, wrapped in cotton wool. Mum fetched some little flowers from the garden and put them in with her, and Bloggs drew a cross on a card and wrote, 'Here lies Chuchi, the Beloved.'

We dug a hole and placed her inside. The ground was hard. It hadn't rained for a long time.

Dad came home, face pale, anger gone.

'I loved the little rat,' he said.

Mum stirred. 'We ought to go and see if Arthur's all right. He must have been terrified when Dennis came out of nowhere and seized Chuchi.'

We all trooped up to my bedroom, and Arthur was there, nervous and jittery; not surprising. Bloggs felt in the dark room Dad had built on above the cage, as a nursery, still crying.

'Now there'll never be any babies,' and then:

'I can feel something. There's something here. The babies!'

'Let me see!' we all cried.

But we couldn't, for it had been made specially dark and quiet for the babies and the only way to see inside was to take the top off.

I fetched the screwdriver. Dad unscrewed the screws. Bloggs chewed her fingers. It seemed to take hours, but at last, there they lay, naked, pink, squirming, beautiful, four of them.

'But how can they survive,' Mum whispered, 'without Chuchi to feed them? I can't feed anything as small as that. They'll starve . . .'

Dad's face had turned even paler. Bloggs was crying again.

'No, I'll put them to sleep first,' he said.

At that moment Arthur jumped out of my hand, where I'd been stroking him for comfort, and ran across the room. We watched him. Perhaps Bloggs isn't so stupid as I've been saying all along, for she got it first.

'Look! Look! That's not Arthur! The tail's too long and the nose is too big, and he's . . . she's heading for the babies! Dennis killed Arthur, not Chuchi! It's Chuchi! She's alive!'

Chuchi had reached the cage and the babies. She pulled them to her, and then all her blue and pink toilet paper, covered herself and the babies with it, and sat, glaring out of the heap, very angrily indeed, as if she didn't think much of us.

We were all grinning from ear to ear.

'Everything's going to be all right. The babies will live now.'

'I'll put the roof back on so that they can be quiet,' Dad said.

As he screwed in the screws, he started to laugh, a funny sort of laugh.

'What is it, Dad?'

'It's just that, well, poor old Arthur – he didn't have much of a life because Chuchi bullied him all the time, and when he dies he gets buried with someone else's name over him, and all of us smiling and happy because he's dead and not Chuchi. Poor old Arthur, I say.'

'Poor Arthur,' we all echoed, but we still didn't feel sad. Chuchi and the babies were going to live. Everything would be all right. Except for Arthur. Poor Arthur.

This story is by Gene Kemp.

The Cat who Lived in a Drainpipe

Three hundred years ago, in the times when men wore swords and rode on horses, when ladies carried fans and travelled in carriages, when ships had sails, and kings lived in castles, and you could buy a large loaf of bread for a penny, there lived three cats in Venice.

Venice is a very peculiar town, built on about a hundred islands. The streets in between the houses are full of water, and are called canals. Only in the narrowest alleys and lanes can you walk on dry ground. If you want to go across town you take a boat called a gondola. If a housewife wants to visit her neighbour on the other side of the street, she has to row herself over, unless there is a bridge by her house. Children and cats in Venice learn to swim almost as soon as they learn to walk.

The three cats I am going to tell you about were called Nero, Sandro, and Seppi.

Nero was large, and pitch-black, and very tough

indeed. His master was a chimney-sweep called Benno Fosco. Nero helped with the sweeping. In Venice, chimneys are swept from above. The sweep, standing on the roof, lets down a long bunch of twigs like a witch's broom to knock out the soot. Nero and his master climbed all over the roofs of Venice with their brooms and their bags full of soot. If a chimney was narrow, or very choked up, Nero would go down first, at top speed, like a diver, boring out the soot with his sharp claws and his powerful paws, and sweeping it loose behind him with his strong whiplike tail.

It was lucky that Nero was black, so that the soot didn't show on his fur; he was always absolutely wadded with soot, and left a cloud of it behind him as he walked about. And if his master gave him a pat, out came another black cloud. No-one, apart from Benno Fosco, would ever have dared to stroke Nero; he might have bitten the finger off anybody who tried. When the chimney-sweep poled his gondola along the canals, loaded with sacks of soot, Nero sat on one of the bags, right at the front, looking like a big fat figurehead carved out of coal. Mostly he stayed silent, but every once in a while he let out a single low, threatening howl: Ow-wow-ow-ow-ow! meaning, Does anybody feel like a fight? And when he did this, the other cats along the waterside, sitting on windowsills or doorsteps or on bridges or other boats, would half close their eyes, and shrug, and keep quite quiet until he had gone by. Nobody ever felt inclined to fight with Nero.

Sandro was quite a different kind of cat. His long, soft fur was a dark orange colour, like a French marigold. His expression was always calm and sleepy and very refined; he spent most of his days dozing on a red velvet cushion in the boudoir of his mistress, who was a princess and lived in a palace in one of the grandest streets. Two or three times a day the princess used to comb Sandro with a silver comb. While doing so she would exclaim admiringly, '*Bello* Sandro! *Bello gatto!*' (*Gatto* means a cat. *Bello* means beautiful.) Sandro never paid the least attention to this, but merely went on dozing harder than ever, with his nose pushed well in under his tail. The only exercise he took during the hours of daylight was an occasional spell of washing. But at night, when his mistress, the Princess Cappella, was asleep, he went out, over the roofs of Venice.

Seppi, the third cat, was quite different again from either of the others. For a start, he was much smaller. Seppi belonged to nobody, he had been born in a worm-eaten fish-basket, and he lived in a broken drainpipe. His mother, unfortunately, had fallen off a fishing-boat and been drowned when he was a kitten; from that day on, Seppi never grew any bigger. He lived on fish-heads and mouldy scraps of macaroni stolen from garbage heaps. He was an ugly little cat, black and white in patches of different sizes, with one black paw and three white, a black mask across his white face, and a saddle of black from shoulders to tail. One ear was black with a white lining, and one white with a black tip; one eye was yellow, and one blue. Also he had suffered from a mishap to his tail: most of it was missing, leaving only a short black stump. This made him look like a rabbit, and ruined his balance. Where other cats could leap gracefully on to narrow ledges, or walk easily along slender rails, Seppi had to concentrate with all his might, or he was liable to overshoot, and topple off edges. But he practised at balancing most patiently; and when he did fall he always landed lightly; he was so skinny that he weighed little more than a duster. Every day he clambered gaily and dangerously all over the roofs and walls and pinnacles and boats and bridges of Venice; he was always hungry but he was always hopeful too, and full of energy and curiosity; people laughed at him and shouted 'Pulchinello' as he went trotting by on his own business because, in his black mask, he looked so like a clown.

These three cats, Nero, Sandro, and Seppi, were not precisely friends. Nero was too tough to need friends, and Sandro too lazy. And both were inclined to look down their noses at Seppi, who was such a common little gutter cat, and so much younger and smaller as well.

But one bond joined all three of them together, and that was music. They were all passionately fond of it. Regularly, every Friday evening, they assembled together for a singing session. They always met in the same place, on a wooden hump-backed bridge over a quiet backwater. And there, all night, in all weather except snow, they would hold their concert, until the first light of the rising sun began to dapple the canal water like pink lettuce leaves.

This was why Nero and Sandro were prepared to tolerate Seppi, and overlook his clownlike appearance and vulgar ways and lack of tail; for in spite of his being so small, he had a remarkably loud voice, and furthermore he could sing higher up the scale than any other cat in Venice.

Their programme of singing was always the same. Nero began, because his voice was the deepest. Squatting on the top step of the bridge, like a big shapeless black lump, with elbows and whiskers sticking out sideways, he would slowly let out four or five howls, all on the same deep, gritty, throbbing bass note, like an old mill-wheel creaking: *How, row, row, row, row, row*.

Then there would be a long, silent pause, until Sandro was ready to sing his part of the trio, which was a slow, sorrowful, wailing, tenor cry, not unlike the hoot of a ship's siren a great way off in the fog.

After that, all three cats would sit silent and motionless, without even the twitch of a whisker, for so great a stretch of time that any listener might be fooled into thinking that they had finished their concert and gone home to bed. But not a bit of it – all of a sudden little Seppi would let out such an ear-piercingly shrill scream – *Freeeeeeeeeeeee!* – that birds, even at dead of night, would wake and twitter in protest under the eaves of nearby houses, dogs would bark for two miles around, while any person walking rather close to a canal in that district would almost certainly be so startled that they would fall into the water. (Fortunately the inhabitants of Venice are quite used to such accidents and think nothing of it.) Even Sandro and Nero never became completely accustomed to Seppi's shriek; each time, after he had sung his part, they would gaze at him almost respectfully for a few moments.

After that, they would repeat the recital, always in the same order, with Nero singing first and Seppi coming in at the end, and long pauses in between the solo parts. At the very end, there would be a short chorus, with all singing together.

Very occasionally, a strange cat might make an attempt to join their group, but neither Sandro nor Nero would dream of permitting this. Sandro would let out a terrifying hiss, Nero would shoot from his place on the top step and give the impertinent candidate such a clip on the ear with a sooty paw that he would fly for his life and think himself lucky to escape with his ears and tail.

In this way the concerts were held, every Friday night. Half the cats of Venice came to listen, and sat in admiring silence at a respectful distance.

Then, at sunrise, the three singers would silently part and go their various ways, Nero flitting over the rooftops to the first job of the day, Seppi trotting off through a network of narrow lanes and alleys, where he might hope to find a fish-tail or a couple of inches of cast-off spaghetti, while Sandro would gracefully wave his golden tail and summon a boat to take him back to the palace where he lived. All the gondoliers who plied their boats for hire along the Venetian canals knew the Princess Cappella and her cat; Sandro never had the least trouble in finding a gondola to take him home; any boatman who picked him up knew that a fee of three golden ducats would be paid without question by the butler who opened the door.

So matters went on for many months.

But one Friday evening in a cold November, when Sandro and Nero reached the bridge at their usual hour, they were surprised to see that Seppi was not there. Usually he was first at the meeting-place, having nothing to do apart from hunting for scraps in the gutters, whereas Nero might be kept late sweeping a chimney, and Sandro might have been obliged to accompany his mistress on a round of calls.

'Where can the little wretch have got to?' Sandro said impatiently, after they had waited for ten minutes. He shivered, for an icy wind was blowing. 'I wish he'd hurry up. There's nothing to beat music for warming you.'

'Shall we start without him?' suggested Nero.

'No, it would be hopeless without the treble part. I do trust the little fool hasn't been kicked into a canal and drowned.'

'More likely got into a fight with someone bigger than himself and had his head bitten off,' said Nero uneasily. 'Now I come to think about it, I haven't seen him around the streets for the last few days.'

'No, it's all right – here he comes,' said Sandro in relief, noticing a small black-and-white shape slip along the top of a wall.

Seppi trotted up the steps to join his fellow-singers. But he did not seem quite his usual care-free self. He offered no explanation as to why he was late, he made no apologies, even when Nero growled at him and Sandro let out a reproving hiss, but sat in silence, with his feet apart and mouth open, staring up dreamily and absent-mindedly at the small frozen-looking moon that floated over-head. Furthermore, when it came to his turn to sing, he waited so long that both his companions began to wonder anxiously if he had lost his voice. And when he did at last let out his screech, it was nothing like so loud and shattering as usual; in fact it was quite a soft plaintive note, not much louder than the cry of a gull, and both Nero and Sandro were quite disgusted by it.

'Come on, sing up, you good-for-nothing!' said Nero, giving him a box on the ear. 'What kind of a noise is *that*? A newborn kitten would do better. Why, a person could hardly hear it across the canal.'

'Are you sick?' inquired Sandro, more sym-pathetically.

'No, no,' murmured Seppi in a vague manner, still staring at the moon.

'Well then, kindly pull yourself together!' said Nero sharply.

After that, Seppi did pull himself together, and sang even better than usual, so well, in fact, that dogs barked all the way to the village of Mestre, and the other two forgot his strange behaviour.

But next week they had cause to remember it again, for he arrived even later than on the previous Friday, and in a most peculiar state, with his whiskers dangling downwards, far-away eyes narrowed to slits, and a layer of dust and cobwebs all over his fur.

Moreover, when it came to his turn to sing, all he could let out was a faint squeak, hardly louder than the noise made by a bat.

'Look here, this is useless!' said Nero in disgust. 'Come on – you'll have to tell us what's up. Where have you been all week? I haven't seen you since last Friday. Where are you spending your time these days?'

'Yes, speak up, Seppi,' added Sandro. 'You owe it to us to tell us what's happened. After all, we taught you all the music you know.'

At that, Seppi was suddenly galvanized; his far-away look vanished, his stump of a tail and scanty whiskers bristled, and he burst into speech.

'Music?' he said. 'Oh, my dear partners, you think we are producing good music here? You think our trio makes the best music in Venice? Just come with me. I'll take you where you can hear something that will make you realize we don't know the first thing about music!'

At this, Nero and Sandro exchanged glances. The little fellow must have gone crazy, their eyes and ears and whiskers suggested. Sandro elegantly shrugged his tail. Oh well, we'll have to humour him. Perhaps we can get him out of this nonsensical fit somehow. Otherwise we'd better start looking for another treble. Too bad.

Anyway, they followed him.

Seppi bolted down the balustrade of the bridge, and along the path beside the canal. Then he led the way at a gallop through twisting alleys, across paved squares, over bridges, along quaysides, until they had come to a much grander and richer part of the town.

Here, Seppi went upwards – up on to a gate, along a wall, on to a roof, and from there in a long leap across an alley on to a higher roof.

'Why are you bringing us here?' said Nero. 'I know this house – it belongs to a wealthy paper manufacturer. I've often swept the chimneys. Once the mistress gave me a whole bowlful of fresh sardines.'

'Yes, yes, I daresay – come along,' said Seppi inattentively, and he led them up and up, towards an attic window. 'Now – come up here and keep quiet and listen!'

The window was a kind of dormer, right in the middle of the roof. All three cats perched on the sill, which was very dusty. It was only a few feet above the level of the flat roof (and this was lucky, for Seppi was in such an excited state that he kept losing his balance and toppling off the edge). 'Now, listen, listen!' he begged again, breathlessly.

Nero and Sandro peered through the window, to see what had made their young colleague so excited. They were looking down into a smallish attic, containing nothing save a chair, a box, a music-stand. On the box lay an oboe. On the chair sat a young man, who was tuning a violin, and a minute or two after they had settled on the sill, he began to play it.

As he played, Nero's and Sandro's eyes became larger and larger, rounder and rounder. Presently Nero surreptitiously wiped a tear off his black nose with the back of his paw. Sandro was soon so overcome by emotion that he had to bury his face in his bushy golden tail. As for Seppi – his blue eye and his yellow one were shining like a sapphire and a topaz respectively.

'There!' he whispered, in a pause. 'Did you ever hear anything as beautiful as that? Ever in your *life*?'

Speechlessly, they shook their heads. They were quite choked with wonder and awe, both at the skill of the player, and the magic of the music.

'There!' said Seppi again, when the player had finished his piece. 'What did I tell you? Now do you see why I have been a bit absent-minded lately? I've spent the whole of every day just sitting on this windowsill, listening to him play.'

'Who is the young man?' inquired Sandro graciously, when he had recovered himself a little.

'I know him,' said Nero. 'He is the paper-manufacturer's son. His name is Tomaso. Once, when I had gone down the chimney and come out into a big saloon downstairs, I heard his father say to him, "Tomaso, my son, music is a fine thing, but why don't you ever go out and amuse yourself like the other young men? Why spend all your days playing your fiddle up there in the attic?" And the mother said to her husband, "Oh, leave the boy alone, Antonio! If he wants to play his fiddle and his oboe, that's a harmless hobby for a young man, and not at all expensive."'

Now the young man began to play again, on the oboe this time, and the tunes he played were so supremely beautiful that Sandro was soon heaving with silent sobs, thinking of his childhood, while Nero fairly burst out boohooing, and had to run twice round the dormer to recover himself. Both of them thanked Seppi from the bottom of their hearts for having given them the chance of such a musical treat.

From that time on, there were no more concerts

on the bridge. Not Friday night only, but every evening of the week was spent by the three partners perched on the dusty sill, listening wide-eyed and open-mouthed to the music made by young Tomaso in his attic. Their own music-making was entirely abandoned; all the cats in Venice wondered what had become of the famous trio, and grieved at their loss. Indeed, another trio of cats had the impudence to take over the wooden bridge but their singing was so inferior that the whole audience joined together to chase them off; and from that time on, Friday nights in that quarter were no different from any other; the people in the houses round about were not sorry, but the cat population thought it a sad loss.

During daylight, of course, Nero and Sandro were obliged to return to their usual occupations, which they did most reluctantly. Benno Fosco soon began to grumble that Nero's chimney-sweeping was becoming very hasty and careless; the Princess Cappella complained that her pet's fur was disgracefully dusty and neglected; and little Seppi gave such scanty attention to hunting for scraps of food that he grew as thin as a withered leaf. He stayed on the windowsill all day long unless young Tomaso went out for a short airing. When he did so, Seppi would hastily scramble down from the roof and try to follow him, either slipping along behind through the lanes and squares, or nipping on board his gondola where, perched in some cranny, he would watch the young man with unblinking love and admiration.

'Oh,' he often thought sadly to himself, 'how happy I would be if only I could belong to him, as Sandro does to the Princess. How proud I would be to sit on the prow of his boat as it glided along the canal.' Or he would imagine lying on a blue velvet cushion in a warm room, listening to his master play for hours together. Surely life could hold no greater happiness than that.

'Still,' he thought, 'I might as well put such ideas out of my head. He could have the handsomest cat in Venice. He'd never look at an ugly little character like me.'

In fact, once or twice, young Tomaso had noticed Seppi stowed in a corner of his gondola and had called to the gondolier. 'Is that cat yours?' 'No, sir, that's little Seppi. He belongs nowhere – he's nobody's cat.' 'How did he get on board?' The boatman would shrug. 'Well, throw him off – he's probably full of fleas!'

Seppi was quite resigned to being thrown off the boat, if discovered, and would simply return to the attic windowsill and wait for Tomaso to come back.

Due to this habit of following the young man

and listening to his conversation, Seppi was better informed about the family's affairs than the other two partners.

Two or three months later there came a violent quarrel between Tomaso and his father, which ended in the young man rushing up to the attic and slamming the door. The father hardly ever climbed above the first floor, where the grand reception rooms were, but on this occasion he came storming up after his son.

'If that's your last word,' he shouted through the door, 'you can just stay in the attic till you change your mind.' And he locked the door and pocketed the key.

Tomaso made no reply.

'I shall tell the servants not to let you have any food or drink until you get this ridiculous notion out of your head!' shouted old Antonio furiously.

Tomaso answered nothing.

'And you needn't think you can talk your mother round, for I'm taking her off to stay with Auntie Gabriella in the country!' roared the old man, and he stamped away downstairs.

'What's all that about?' said Sandro to Seppi (for it was evening, and all three cats were there). 'What has young Tomaso done that's so upset the old man?'

'He has fallen in love with a girl at one of the orphanages. He wants to marry her.'

(There were four big orphanages in Venice, where the orphans were all taught music and learned to sing most beautifully.)

'*Dio mio!*' said Nero. 'What possessed him to do that? I thought the orphans were all bow-legged or one-eyed?'

'Not this one,' said Seppi. 'I've seen Tomaso meet her. She is very pretty. And she has a fine singing voice. Her name is Margherita.'

'Well then why won't his father let Tomaso marry her?'

'He wants his son to marry some rich girl.'

'Humph,' said Sandro. 'I daresay Tomaso will give in, when he begins to feel really hungry.'

'If he had any gumption he'd escape over the roof,' said Nero.

'He could never do it,' said Seppi. 'A cat could, but not a human.'

It was true that the house was extremely high; the roof commanded a beautiful view over half Venice, but there was no way down, except for cats. Next morning young Tomaso found that out for himself; he climbed out of his window, walked round the roof inspecting its possibilities, and then, shrugging, returned to the attic, where he spent the day composing and playing the most heart-rending tunes.

'The parents have gone off to the country,' reported Seppi when Sandro and Nero arrived that evening. 'And they took all the servants with them except for a very bad-tempered steward, who has orders not to allow Tomaso any food until he writes a letter to his father promising to stop thinking about the girl.'

Indeed at that moment they heard the steward, whose name was Michele, banging on the attic door.

'Will you write to your father and say you have changed your mind?'

'Never!' shouted the young man, and he blew a defiant blast on his oboe.

'Then you get no supper,' said Michele, and they heard his footsteps retreating down the stairs.

Two days went by.

'This is becoming serious,' said Sandro. 'The young man is growing so pale and thin. Humans have to eat a lot in order to survive. Suppose he should die? No more music!'

Even Nero looked grave at this, and little Seppi nearly fell off the windowsill at such a dreadful idea. During the next day, with terrible difficulty, because of his poor balance, he lugged up two large fish-heads on to the roof, and laid them hopefully on the windowsill. But the prisoner inside did not seem to notice them. After another night, Tomaso just lay all day on his cloak, which was spread on the floor; he seemed to be very weak and did not play on his violin, though he occasionally blew a few notes on his oboe.

'A terrible thing has happened!' reported Seppi agitatedly, when Sandro and Nero arrived on the following evening.

'What now?'

'That steward – Michele – he got mixed up in a fight with some sailors on the quayside. I was watching from the garden wall. A stone hit him on the head, and he was carried off as if he were dead.'

'So now nobody in Venice knows that the poor young man is starving in the attic?' said Sandro.

'*Dio mio* – that's bad,' said Nero.

'It's up to us to do something about him,' said Seppi.

'But what?' said Sandro.

All three sat racking their brains.

'He needs food,' said Nero, after a lot of thought.

'He didn't see the fish-heads I brought him,' said Seppi sadly.

'*Fish-heads* are no use,' said Sandro with scorn. 'Humans don't eat that kind of stuff.'

There was another long, worried silence.

'If only we could get through the window,' said Seppi.

But it was tight shut. All their poking and prying had no effect. And the young man was lying with his back to them, without moving, as if he were very weak indeed.

At last Seppi said, looking rather embarrassed, 'I think I have had an idea.'

'Well, what is it?' said Nero. 'Come on – speak up.'

'Well,' Seppi said, more and more bashful, as the other two waited expectantly, 'I have a – a sort of friend; he – he occupies the other end of the drainpipe where I live.'

'Who is this person?'

Nero and Sandro exchanged looks and shrugs. Evidently it was some frightfully low connection – though what alley-cat could be even lower down the social scale than Seppi, it was hard to imagine.

'His name is Umberto,' muttered Seppi, blushing under his fur.

'Never heard of him. I thought I knew all the cats in Venice,' said Nero.

'Umberto isn't – isn't exactly a cat.'

'Well? What is he?'

'He's – he's a – a m-mouse.'

'*What?*' Nero and Sandro nearly fell off the sill in their outrage and disapproval.

'A highly intelligent mouse, of course,' Seppi went on hastily, gabbling in his anxiety; 'he saved my life once, when I had a fish-bone stuck in my throat. He pulled it out.'

'Well?' demanded Nero after another awful

silence. 'What is your idea in regard to this *mouse*?'

'Don't you see?' Seppi picked up courage a little. 'Mice can get *into* places. If I brought Umberto here – but you would have to promise to – to respect his advisory position – he could probably nibble a way into the attic. And he could carry in food.'

'What sort of food could *he* take?' said Sandro scornfully.

Seppi had been thinking hard about this.

'Well – cheese. Peas. Things that a mouse can carry.'

'Humph,' said Nero. 'Yes. It's a possibility I will admit. Anyway, there's no use discussing what he could carry until we have met – this character, and he has surveyed the situation. Could you fetch him here, Seppi?'

'I could try.'

'Trying is not good enough. I had better come with you,' said Sandro. 'You have such a wretched sense of balance; it would be disastrous if you dropped – this person, on your way here. I'm sure he's the only mouse in Venice who has ever got into conversation with a cat.'

'All right; come along if you think so,' agreed Seppi doubtfully. 'But you will be careful with him, won't you?'

'Honour of a Cappella. I've often carried out the kitchen cat's kittens when they get into my mistress's boudoir. I know all about handling.'

Seppi was so worried about Tomaso that he wasn't particularly embarrassed at taking Sandro to his humble home. His mind was occupied with the problem of what food could be transported to the attic. Eggs? Could mice carry eggs? Carrots? Meatballs?

Umberto was a large stocky brown mouse, with flashing black eyes, and a grey muzzle, whiskers, and tail, for he was fairly advanced in years. Seppi had already told him about the poor young man's plight, so he was not greatly astonished when the two cats arrived at his end of the drainpipe and asked if he would come with them – though he did not look altogether happy at the prospect of being carried there in Sandro's mouth.

However, Sandro proved to be a careful and reliable bearer; in record time he carried Umberto back over the walls and rooftops as delicately as if he had had a peacock's egg between his jaws; Umberto certainly had a more comfortable ride than he would have done if Seppi had carried him by the scruff of his neck; though Seppi did wonder, when they arrived at the attic windowsill, if Umberto's whiskers had not gone a shade or two whiter.

Nevertheless, the minute he was set down, the mouse began to bustle about the windowsill, surveying its possibilities in a thoroughly professional manner.

'Why, this will be quite easy,' he said. 'In fact there is already a mousehole through the wooden window-frame; it has been blocked with putty and scraps of paper but I can clear that out in fifteen minutes.'

And he began briskly nibbling with his razor-sharp teeth, and scooping out the debris with his tiny but strong and skilful paws.

The other three sat watching and wishing they could do something helpful.

'Why don't you fetch some food while I do this?' Umberto suggested when he came out of his tunnel for a mouthful of fresh air.

This seemed a good idea. Sandro and Nero left at once. But Seppi said that he would remain behind and help.

'When you have made the hole just a little bigger I can poke in my paw and bring out the loose stuff.'

In ten minutes Nero and Sandro returned, Nero with a hunk of parmesan cheese, Sandro carrying half a long thin loaf of bread. They had stolen these things from a trattoria at the end of the street.

'Excellent,' said Umberto, who was gaining more confidence as he became used to the situation. 'Now – if Seppi can poke in his paw once more, I think it will be possible to push the rest of the barrier through into the attic.'

Seppi thrust his paw in up to the shoulder

and managed to shift the rest of the stopping; then Umberto ran through the tunnel.

'All clear,' he reported, coming back. 'And the young man is asleep, not dead; he's breathing, but his eyes are shut.'

Meanwhile the others had been nibbling off small scraps of cheese and bread, of a suitable size to be taken in through the hole. Umberto carried some of them in and laid them beside the young man. His report was unpromising, however.

'He doesn't seem to want to wake up and eat them. Humans are so sluggish! If you put delicious strong-smelling cheese beside a sleeping mouse, he would be awake in a moment.'

'Could you lay a crumb or two on his mouth?' suggested Seppi.

Umberto tried.

'No good,' he came back to say presently. 'The young man just brushes them off with his hand. And his head is as hot as a fire. I think he has a fever.'

'When my mistress had a fever,' said Sandro, 'she ate a lot of fruit. Oranges and melons.'

'*Melons?* How are we going to carry *melons* up here?' said Nero irritably.

'I have an idea!' said Seppi. 'Grapes! And I know where there are some, too. Down below, at the back of this house, there is a big glass room – sometimes I come up that way over its roof – and inside there is a vine covered with grapes. Umberto – couldn't you go down inside the house and fetch some – or ask the house-mice to help? There must be plenty inside somewhere – every house in Venice is full of mice.'

'I will see if it can be done,' said Umberto. And he disappeared back through the tunnel. Presently he pushed his head out to announce that it was possible to squeeze under the attic door and he intended to go on a voyage of exploration. He vanished again and did not return for a long time.

By now the night was nearly past. Roosters were crowing in back yards, and all the domes and pinnacles of Venice were beginning to turn pink. Nero and Sandro reluctantly went off to their day's duties.

'But we'll come back this evening,' they promised.

'Bring some food when you come,' begged Seppi. 'Or some drink.'

'*Drink?* How do you expect us to do that?'

But then Sandro reflected. 'My mistress has a leather wine-bottle that's not too big. I might be able to carry it. But how shall we get it into the attic? It's far too large to go through that hole.'

'Perhaps Umberto can make the hole bigger before you come back. Or I can. I'll work at it all day.'

After they had gone Seppi worked on a plan of his

own. Umberto's opening of the passage had slightly loosened the bottom left-hand window-pane. Seppi pushed his paw into the mousehole and worked it from side to side, shoving with his shoulder against the loose pane, which rattled and shifted and gave, little by little. But it was slow, hard, tiring work; he wished that Umberto would come back and help by nibbling away the putty round the edge of the pane. Seppi tried to do this himself, but his teeth were not the right shape. He went back to pushing and poking. After a couple more hours of this – all of a sudden, triumph! – the pane fell inward on to the floor with a tinkling crash.

It was a very small pane, however. Seppi wondered if he would be able to squeeze through the square hole that it had left. I shall look a real fool if I get stuck halfway, he thought, and tried his whiskers for size. They fitted – exactly. Holding his breath, Seppi wriggled through. He could just do it, due to his extra thinness from the last few days of anxiety.

At last he was in the attic where he had so often longed to be! It's lucky I'm small, he reflected; neither Nero nor Sandro could have done it.

He crept across the floor to where Tomaso lay on the cloak, and sniffed the young man all over. Alive, thank goodness! – but Umberto was right: Tomaso was certainly sick; his hands and forehead were burning hot, his lips were dry and cracked, and he tossed from side to side, muttering in his feverish dream: '*Mamma!* Please don't punish me. I played that last piece too fast, I must play it again slower. Margherita, why won't you come to see me? Please look this way —'

Seppi was greatly distressed at being able to do so little for his hero. He licked Tomaso's forehead all over several times, in hopes of cooling it a little; he fetched in some more of the bread and cheese from outside, but it was plain that the young man was too seriously ill to benefit from this kind of food.

At last, to his great relief, Seppi heard a soft snuffling and scraping from the other side of the attic door, and turned in time to see Umberto squeeze underneath, rolling in front of him a large green grape. He was followed by a second mouse – a third – a fourth – a fifth – each of them had brought a grape. More and more mice came pouring in, until the attic floor was quite covered with mice, and grapes were rolling about everywhere.

'Oh, bravo, bravo! Well done, my dear, dear friend!' exclaimed Seppi joyfully. 'Now, if only we can get the young man to eat one of the grapes —'

Easier said than done, however. Seppi tried dropping the grapes on to Tomaso's mouth. But, like the bread and cheese crumbs, they only rolled off. 'And, in any case, he might choke if one went into his throat,' pointed out Umberto. 'Like you with the fish-bone, Seppi.'

At last they solved the problem. Working together, two of the mice, one seated on Tomaso's collar and one on his cheekbone, managed to squeeze a grape so that its juice ran into the corner of the patient's open mouth.

'He swallowed!' cried Seppi. 'I saw his throat move. Quickly! Another grape!'

In no time they had a relay system working – grapes were passed from paw to paw, as fast as drops of rain running down a railing. When, fairly soon, the two grape squeezers became exhausted, with aching paws and heaving chests, they were replaced by two others. Mice rushed to and fro, under the door, down the stairs to the hot-house where the vine grew. The patient swallowed and swallowed, always with his eyes shut.

At last he gave a deep sigh and shut his mouth tight, so that the juice from the last grape ran over his chin. Then he turned over, burying his face in his folded arm; two of the mouse-squeezers narrowly avoided being squashed.

'I think he has had enough for now,' said Umberto. 'Sick people should not have much at a time. But I believe the grapes have done good.'

It was true that the young man was breathing more easily. His head was not so hot, and he had stopped talking in his sleep. The mice ran all over him sympathetically.

'*Poverino!* Poor young man. It is a shame. His parents should not treat him so. Such a handsome young fellow too!'

'I expect they did not mean him to die,' Seppi said. 'They believe the steward is here to keep an eye on him.'

'But he is not! He has never come back. Downstairs the house is quite empty.'

'Is there any food about?'

'Some; not a lot. What should we bring up?'

'Anything you can carry.'

So, during the rest of the day, there was a continuous come-and-go of mice, up and down the stairs, and under the attic door, with all the food they could find and carry: nuts, olives, dried cherries, beans, brussels sprouts, grains of rice, more grapes, small pieces of carrot, of artichoke, of cheese, of dried fish.

Seppi sat by the young man, lovingly licking and relicking his forehead all day, over and over, until his tongue became quite tired and dry. Twice more Tomaso half-woke, and was given more grape-juice each time by relays of helpful mice.

After dark, Nero and Sandro returned. They were staggering with fatigue. Between them, taking it in turns, they had carried up a heavy leather bottle.

73

'*Dio mio!*' Nero said. 'It will be days before my neck muscles recover from carrying that thing. But I think we can just squeeze it through the hole. What a lucky thing that you managed to get that pane out.'

Nero and Sandro pushed; Seppi gripped the neck of the flask and pulled; at last it fell through on to the floor.

'What's in it? Wine?'

'No, much better,' said Sandro. 'Teriaca! My mistress got it from a witch.'

Teriaca was a kind of medicine much used in Venice at that time. It was made from cinnamon, pepper, fennel, rose-leaves, amber, gum arabic, opium, and many other herbs and spices. It was supposed to cure everything except the plague.

'How are we going to get the cork out?'

The mice were equal to that. They soon had the cork nibbled away.

Now came a difficulty though. Even Seppi and the mice together were not strong enough to hoist up the bottle to Tomaso's mouth – and there was a great danger, as they pushed and pulled, that all the precious contents would be spilled. Nero and Sandro, watching through the window, shouted advice but couldn't get in to help; the hole was too small for either of them to climb through. 'Prop his head on the violin. No, on the oboe.' But this proved impossible.

'Well, we'll have to use drastic measures,' Seppi announced, and, ordering the mice to keep the bottle tipped upwards, as close to the young man's face as possible, he bit Tomaso's hand sharply.

Roused by the sudden pain, the young man opened his eyes and saw the bottle right in front of them.

'I'm dreaming – dreaming . . .' he murmured, but he raised himself on one elbow, grasped the bottle, and drank off its powerful-smelling contents in one long swallow. Then he fell back again and shut his eyes.

'*Bravo, bravo!*' cried the mice. 'Now he will be better! The teriaca will cure him! All we need do is keep him fed, and soon we shall be hearing his beautiful music again.

'And, now his large excellency the Great Black Cat is here, perhaps your honour wouldn't mind coming down to the kitchen and taking the lid off the big iron pot there – we know it is full of cooked spaghetti which the steward made before he went away, but the lid is too heavy for us to shift. Your Magnificence will be able to do it easily.'

Nero was rather affronted at being given orders by the mice, although they had been very polite about it. He stared at them sharply to make sure they were not poking fun at him.

'How do you suggest I get into the kitchen?' he said coldly.

'Why, *ebbene*, down the chimney of course! *Il signore* Nero knows better than anyone in Venice how to do *that*. The fire is out – since many days.'

'Yes, that does seem a good idea, Nero,' Sandro remarked. 'And while you are down in the kitchen you might find other kinds of food that the mice can't reach.'

'You won't be *unkind* to any of the mice while you are down there, will you?' Seppi said anxiously. 'They are working so hard to save Tomaso.'

Nero promised to restrain himself, and went off to the chimney-stack, which was at the other side of the roof. They heard a heaving and thumping; then nothing more. A considerable time passed.

Sandro began to worry.

'I do hope he has not got stuck in the chimney. After all, it is different when his master is there with brushes and ropes.'

But presently mice began to emerge from under the door, dragging immense lengths of spaghetti which they had hauled all the way up the stairs from the kitchen. Soon a large, pale pile of it was coiled up in one corner of the attic. From some scuffles and a few curses on the other side of the door, it could be guessed that Nero was helping in this operation, but was finding it hard to co-operate with the mice.

After a while he reappeared outside the window, dragging a bunch of very sooty dried sausages which he pushed through the hole.

'There wasn't much else in the kitchen,' he reported. 'I daresay the family took most of the food with them when they went to the country. We'll have to arrange for a supply of food from outside.'

Since the prisoner was now well supplied for the moment, however, with enough to last him at least for a couple of days, and since everybody was tired out, the mice limped off to their quarters downstairs, and Nero and Sandro prepared to go home. Seppi said that he would spend the night with the patient. Umberto asked, rather diffidently, if someone could take him home, as it was rather a long journey and he was not certain of the way.

'My dear Umberto! Of course I shall see you back to your door,' Sandro said graciously.

In consequence of which, an amazed late-night gondolier, poling his craft home along the Grand Canal, found himself beckoned to the quayside by a negligent wave of Sandro's golden tail – 'and, would you credit, there was a *mouse* riding on the cat's back!' he reported later to his wife. 'And they *both* got off at the Cappella Palace.'

'Ernesto, you've had too much Chianti again,' said his wife turning over sleepily in bed.

Luckily the drainpipe shared by Seppi and Umberto was only a couple of blocks from the Cappella Palace; Sandro carried Umberto to his door as promised, and went home himself for a well-earned day's sleep. Nero was already curled up on a soot-sack in his master's boat, taking a cat-nap. But Seppi sat up for the rest of the night, watching the sleeping Tomaso and observing with joy, as dawn approached, that the young man's breathing became slower and easier, his brow was cool, his hands were damp, and the fever had left him. At last, satisfied that the patient would recover, Seppi curled up in a ball, comfortably jammed against Tomaso's chest, and they slept together.

They woke together too, for Tomaso, half-way through the morning, suddenly sat up with a strangled shout, dislodging Seppi, who bounced on to his feet with his fur on end.

'What – what am I doing here?' said the young man confusedly. 'I dreamed – I was dreaming I had been alone for days and days – I was starving to death. Was it true? Good heavens,' he added, looking round him at all the little heaps of olives and grapes, the rows of carrots and beans, the tastefully arranged little patterns of cherries and chestnuts, of rice and peas, and the pale heap of spaghetti. 'Who brought all this? Did Michele?'

'Prrrt,' said Seppi.

'Or did you?' said Tomaso, looking at him closely. 'How did *you* find your way in here? I know you – you're the little fellow who's always trying to steal a ride on my gondola. Well, I'm

happy to have your company now, I can tell you
– you are kindly welcome to share my breakfast.'

Seppi did not wish to do this, but watched with
huge satisfaction as the young man made a good
meal of spaghetti and olives, grapes and chestnuts
and sausages.

Presently some of the house-mice arrived to
ask if more supplies were needed yet; they brought
with them small lumps of fresh stracchino cheese.

'Some friends from outside had heard of the
young gentleman's situation, and they sent this in
as they live in a dairy; they wondered if he could
use it.'

Tomaso watched in utter amazement as the procession of mice rolled pieces of cheese across the floor and Seppi supervised their arrangement on an artichoke leaf.

Then a gull tapped at the window.

'Beg pardon – I understand that the young fellow who lives here and plays the violin is in need of a bit of fruit?'

About fifty gulls swooped past, each dropping an orange or a grapefruit on to the roof.

Next a whole flock of pigeons arrived, each bearing some delicacy – a small cake, a shrimp, a sardine.

'We picked these up in the street market,' one of them told Seppi. 'There's a rumour going round among all the mice of the town that the young musician here is starving; we couldn't have that. Everybody loves his playing.'

And a convocation of swans flew by, each bearing an oyster.

'With best wishes for the young gentleman's recovery.'

And a procession of rats came toiling over the rooftops from a spaghetti factory; Tomaso had enough spaghetti to last him a year, piled up on the roof.

'Seppi,' he said in amazement, 'you seem to have the whole town organized.'

Seppi modestly busied himself in washing his stump of tail; he felt that it was unfair he should receive all the credit.

Three or four days passed in this manner – a week – two weeks. Sandro and Nero returned every evening. But Seppi stayed with Tomaso daylong and nightlong; by day he watched contentedly as Tomaso nibbled at his provisions and slowly grew stronger; by night they both slept curled up together under Tomaso's cloak.

At the end of the first week Tomaso was sufficiently recovered to begin playing a few tunes on his oboe. And, at that, Seppi was flooded by such happiness that he hardly knew how to contain himself: to be able to sit, hour after hour, on the musician's cloak, listening to his marvellously beautiful music – what other cat in the world could possibly have such good fortune?

On the fifteenth day a gull flew over, shouting, 'The parents are coming! They are coming along the canal in a gondola!'

Soon there was a confused noise downstairs, of doors opening, and bumps and thumps and loud voices exclaiming in horror.

Then, heavy steps running up the stairs. The mice all bolted for cover.

And suddenly the door flew open, after a rattling of key in lock, and in burst Tomaso's father and mother. Their faces were as white as stracchino cheese – plainly they expected to find their son stretched out dead on the floor.

'My son, my son!'

'My darling child!'

'Oh, my dear boy!'

'*Dio mio*, he is safe, he is alive! Heaven be thanked.'

They embraced Tomaso, over and over. 'Oh, my dear child! By what merciful providence are you still with us?' said his father. 'Where is Michele? What happened? We had told him to let you out after four days, even if you did not change your mind. And we meant to come back at the end of a week – but your mother fell ill, in the country, and we could not leave until yesterday. And we had heard nothing from Michele. What has happened? We found the house empty and all the fires out – *who* has been feeding you all this time?'

'Quite evidently the blessed saints have been looking after the boy,' said his mother, gazing round, with the tears pouring down her face. '*Now* do you see, Antonio, that he is something special, and that if he wants to marry a girl called Margherita from the orphanage – who, I daresay, is a perfectly nice little thing – he should be allowed to do so?'

'Oh, very well,' agreed old Antonio, who, in fact, was so glad to find his dear son still alive that he would have allowed him to marry a mermaid; if one had been at hand. 'But was it really the blessed saints who were looking after you, my dear Tomaso?'

'No, Father. It was an ugly little cat with no tail called Seppi.'

'A *cat*? Where is he?' cried the mother. 'He shall sit on a gold cushion till the end of his days.'

But Seppi, scared by all the noise and excitement, had darted in nervous haste out through the window-hole – thanking his stars that he had eaten only very politely and sparingly of Tomaso's provisions and was still thin enough to squeeze through. No sign of either him or the mice remained – only a room piled high with olives and chestnuts and cheese.

Tomaso's parents practically carried him downstairs; they wanted to feast him on all the finest delicacies in Venice, but he said he was really full up and could eat nothing more just then. So, instead, they sent a note to the orphanage, asking for the hand of Margherita Rimondi for their son and heir. It was arranged that the young couple should be married two weeks from that day.

A couple of days later Tomaso's mother said to him, 'What is the matter, my son? You look thoughtful. Aren't you quite happy?'

'Well, yes, I am, mother, happy as the day is long. But I wish I could find that little cat. I wish he hadn't disappeared. It was really he who saved my life.'

'Are you sure you didn't dream him in the fever, my son?'

'Oh, I do hope I didn't!' said Tomaso. But then he added, 'No, I'm sure I didn't dream him, for I used to find him hiding in my gondola before all this happened.'

'Well, then, it should be possible to find him.'

In the meantime, where *was* Seppi?

Back in his drainpipe. He had fled to his only refuge, feeling sure that, now the young man's family had returned, and all was forgiven, nobody would even spare a thought for a dirty little alley-cat with most of his tail missing.

Day after day, Seppi stayed crouching in the pipe, damp and melancholy, not even bothering to step outside for a breath of fresh air.

'You really ought to take a bit of exercise, you know,' said Umberto disapprovingly, from the other end of the pipe. Seppi merely grunted in reply. He was thinking, 'When Tomaso is married he might move away from Venice. I may never see him any more; never hear him play again.'

He was very miserable.

And then, one day, he heard a gondola swishing along the canal outside his drainpipe, and he heard Nero's deep bass bellow:

'Seppi! Come out of there! Everybody is looking for you!'

Seppi put his head out of the pipe. There was Benno Fosco's boat, full of black sacks, and Nero, sooty, stately, and commanding.

'Come on! Hurry up! Tomaso is getting married tomorrow, and he wants all the friends who helped him when he was a prisoner to join in his wedding procession, and you especially.'

'Oh, he won't miss *me*,' said Seppi, pulling his head back in again.

'What rubbish! Why, he's had notices put up all over Venice: Wanted to find: Small black and white cat with one blue eye, one yellow, and half a tail.'

'*Really?*'

'He wants you to live in his house!'

'Wh-what?'

'And you might just as well,' said Nero kindly, 'I think it's an excellent scheme. After all, Sandro and I have good homes of our own, but what have you got? A drainpipe! What kind of establishment is that? Hurry up – Benno can't wait about all day. We've got six customers to take care of.'

It was an unforgettable wedding. Gulls and pigeons flew over the bridal gondola. Swans drifted after it. Mice lined the quayside and bridges. And all the cats of Venice were there – perched on sills, on doorsteps, on steps, on skiffs and ferries, on hulls and prows. So many cats together were never seen before or since.

Seppi went to live with Tomaso and Margherita. He slept on a blue velvet cushion. He became brilliantly clean, his white patches like silk and his black like ebony. But he never grew any bigger. He played with all the six children of Tomaso and Margherita, as they came along, and his nine lives extended on and on, until they seemed more like ninety-nine. He was happier than any other cat in Italy, for, alone of all the household, he was allowed into the musician's workroom and could listen to every note that his master – who became a famous composer – ever played.

(But on one night a week, Seppi went out over the roofs, and sang in a concert with Sandro and Nero. All the Venetian cats were delighted to have their favourite trio back, and indeed the three became so well known that cats travelled from Milan and even Rome to hear them.)

Several years later, Tomaso, now very famous indeed, was invited to visit the Duke of Bavaria. And, while on this visit, one day in the street, he ran into a man who went chalk-white at the sight of him, fell on his knees, and stammered, 'It's n-n-never the young master? Praise be to all the holy saints! I thought you were dead!'

He was Michele, the steward.

He told how he had been knocked unconscious in a street-fight, and woke to find himself on a ship, where he had been dumped by someone who thought he was a sailor. The ship was already half-way to Africa.

'And when I thought of how you had been left – all alone in the house – oh, I nearly went mad! A week had gone by – I thought you must be dead already. I never dared go back to Venice. I've been in terrible grief all my days, thinking about you, and how your father and mother must have felt when they returned. Oh, forgive me, forgive me!'

'Forgive? It was not your fault!' said Tomaso. 'Quick – jump on a horse and hurry back to Venice! You were only doing what you had been ordered.'

'I was to let you out after four days!'

'So you would have. You didn't mean to leave me shut up in the attic. But anyway – what a good thing you did! For without that, I should never have married. And I would never have found my Seppi!'

Author's note: Tomaso Albinoni, son of a wealthy paper-manufacturer, lived in Venice from 1671 to 1750, wrote beautiful music, married Margherita Rimondi, and had six children. There is no record of his having a cat. But he probably did. Venice is full of cats.

This story is by Joan Aiken.

The Asrai

I have not told this story to many people. I will tell you, but perhaps you should not speak of it to anyone else. It is a strange story and not everyone would believe it. I know the truth.

In the north of the country, there is a great lake. It is clear and deep, and rich in fish, but no-one fishes there. A lake as deep as that has secrets. Every day, the fishermen would go further north, making a longer journey, rather than fish in its still waters. No-one even spoke of the lake until the young man came.

'Are there no fish in the lake?'

'Yes. Good fish, they say, and many of them,' replied the fishermen.

'Then why not fish there instead of going further off?'

Nobody would answer at first. They looked away or spoke of other things. At last, one old man took him aside, speaking quietly.

'The lake you speak of has never been fished by our people. There are stories from the past. It is very deep, very still, fringed with reeds and full of peace. Perfect, in fact, for the Asrai.'

'The Asrai?' asked the young man. 'What do you mean?'

'I have never seen them myself,' said the old man, 'but my grandfather knew something of them. He would never tell us the full story, but I remember his eyes when he said the name – deep, grey and sad like the lake. The Asrai are the people of the lake. They live in its depths, rarely visiting the surface. Their hair is green and their skin sparkles and changes colour like the water. My grandfather said that they do not seek to harm us, and yet he feared them, I think.'

The young man smiled. 'You do not fish a perfectly good lake because your grandfather said there were people living at the bottom? Are you serious? Surely you do not believe such a story!'

'I believe,' said the old man. 'There have been – incidents. Perhaps I should not have told you. The Asrai are dangerous, even to think about. Put all thought of them out of your mind. Come with us to the far lake and be happy.'

But the young man laughed aloud and walked away.

From that time, the young man fished in the great

lake and had wonderful luck. Every night, he would push his boat out through the reeds and glide across the still water. At dawn, he would return, many fish filling his baskets. He had to sell them in the distant town. In the village by the lake, no-one would buy the fish which belonged to the Asrai.

His good fortune lasted all the summer, but one night the air felt sharp and brown leaves lay in his path. The lake was as still as ever but it no longer sparkled. The reeds, stiffened perhaps by a tinge of frost, held him back for a moment as if in warning. But to the young man, it meant nothing. All night long he fished and, as the sky began to pale, he pulled in a loaded net. There seemed to be weed floating in the net, but then the young man understood. He looked closer. It was long, green hair. He had caught an Asrai.

The Asrai was a young woman. Her skin glittered and her hands and feet were delicately webbed. But her eyes! They were deep like the lake, as grey as the coming morning and so sad. He thought she spoke. He could not tell if it was the Asrai or the rippling movement of the lake. In his head, the sound said, 'Let the Asrai go. Return the Asrai to the lake.'

He hesitated, then looked firmly towards the shore. He would be famous. He would show her to everyone and be well paid for it. He no longer thought of the Asrai, only of himself. He leaned

over the side and pulled her aboard. As he did so, a pain scorched his hand. Although her touch was cool, it was almost as if it had burned him. She, too, shrank from his human warmth and the rising sun. Because she seemed to fear the daylight, he threw some reeds over her in the bottom of the boat, and pulled hard for the shore.

He reached the end of the lake just as the sun rose. He felt well satisfied with his catch, and threw off the covering reeds. The Asrai was not there. His net was empty. In the bottom of the boat there was nothing but a pool of lake water.

Ever after, the hand which had touched the Asrai was icy cold, and yet, it was marked, as if it had been passed through fire.

As I say, perhaps we should not speak further of this. These days, people do not know of the Asrai, but I know the truth. If I took off my glove you would understand.

Told from English folk lore by Pat Thomson.

The Cat and the Dog

Once upon a time a man called Simon and his wife Susan lived by the river with their old cat and dog. One day Simon said to Susan, 'Why should we keep that old cat any longer? She can't catch mice any more – in fact she's so slow she's no use to anyone. Why, a whole family of mice might dance on top of her and she wouldn't catch a single one. She's got to go. The next time I see her, I shall drown her in the river.'

Susan was very unhappy when she heard this, and so was the cat, who had been listening behind the stove. When Simon went off to his work, the poor cat miaowed pitifully and looked sadly up into Susan's face. So the woman quickly opened the door and said, 'Run away as fast as you can, puss – quick, before Simon comes home.'

The cat took her advice and ran as quickly as her poor old legs would carry her into the wood. When Simon came home, his wife told him the cat had vanished.

'So much the better for her,' said Simon. 'And now that we're rid of her, we must think what to do with the old dog. He's deaf and blind and is for ever barking when there's no need, and not making a sound when there is. The courtyard might be swarming with thieves and he'd not raise a paw. The next time I see him, I'll hang him.'

When she heard this Susan was very unhappy, and so was the dog, who was lying in the corner of the room and had heard everything. As soon as Simon went off to work, the dog howled so miserably that Susan quickly opened the door, and said, 'Come on, dear, off you go, before Simon gets home.' And the dog ran into the wood. When her husband returned, Susan told him the dog had disappeared.

'Lucky for him,' growled Simon. But Susan was very unhappy, for she had been fond of both her pets, and now they were gone.

Now it happened that the cat and the dog met each other on their travels. Though they hadn't been the best of friends at home, they were glad to meet among strangers. They sat down under a holly tree and talked about how pleasant life had been back at the farm, and how they wished they were back at home. Presently a fox passed by and, seeing the pair together, asked them why they were sitting there and what they were grumbling about.

The cat replied, 'I've caught many a mouse in my day, but now that I'm too old to work, my master wants to drown me.'

And the dog said, 'I've watched and guarded my master's house night after night, and now that I'm too old and deaf, he wants to hang me.'

The fox answered, 'That is the way of the world. I think I can help you both to get back in front of your master's fire. But first, will you help me in *my* troubles?'

They promised to do their best, and the fox explained. 'The wolf has declared war against me, and is at this very moment planning to attack me with the help of the bear and the wild boar. Tomorrow there will be a terrible battle.'

'All right,' said the dog and the cat. 'You can count on our help.' And they shook paws on the bargain. The fox sent word to the wolf to meet him at a certain place, and the three set forth to face him and his friends.

The wolf, the bear and the wild boar arrived first. They waited some time for the fox, until the impatient bear said, 'I'll climb that oak tree, and see if they're coming.'

The first time he looked round, he said, 'I don't see anything.' The second time he looked round, he said, 'I still don't see anything.' But the third time he roared with laughter and said, 'I can see a vast army in the distance, and one of the soldiers has the biggest spear I've ever seen!'

He had spied the cat, who was marching along with her tail on end. Then they all laughed and jeered; but it was so hot that the bear yawned and said, 'The enemy won't be here for hours, so I'll just curl up in the fork of this tree and take a little nap.'

The wolf lay down under the oak, and the wild boar buried himself in some straw so that you could only see one ear. And while they were lying there, the fox, the cat and the dog arrived. When the cat saw the wild boar's ear she pounced on it, thinking it was a mouse in the straw.

The wild boar scrambled up in a dreadful fright, gave one loud grunt, and disappeared into the wood. But the cat was even more startled than the boar. Spitting with terror, she sprang up into the fork of the tree and, as it happened, landed right in the bear's face. Now it was the bear's turn to be in a fright, and with a mighty growl he jumped from the oak, fell right on top of the wolf, and they were both killed. The fox was delighted. 'Right,' he said. 'Now it's time for me to keep *my* part of the bargain.'

On their way home the fox caught a mass of mice, and when they reached Simon's cottage he laid them in a row on the stove. 'Now take one mouse after another,' he told the cat, 'and lay them down in front of your master.'

She did exactly as the fox told her.

When Susan saw this, she said to her husband, 'Just look! Here's our old cat back again – and what a great number of mice she's caught!'

'Wonders will never cease!' cried Simon. 'I certainly never thought that old cat would ever catch another mouse.'

But Susan answered: 'There, you see, I always said she was a wonderful mouser – but you always think you know best.'

Then the fox said to the dog, 'Our friend Simon has just killed a pig and made a string of sausages that just asks to be stolen. When it's a little darker, slip into the courtyard and bark with all your might.'

'All right,' said the dog. And as soon as it was dusk he began to bark loudly.

Susan heard him first and called to her husband, 'Our dog must have come back, for I know his bark. Do go out and see what's the matter. Perhaps someone is stealing our sausages.'

But Simon answered: 'That silly animal's as deaf as a post and is always barking for nothing.' And he stayed put in his chair.

The next morning Susan rose early to go to the nearby town, and thought she would take some sausages to her aunt there. But when she went to her larder, she found all the sausages gone, and a great hole in the floor. She called out to her husband: 'There, I knew I was right. Thieves *were* here last night, and they haven't left a single sausage. Oh, if only you'd gone when I asked you to!'

Then Simon scratched his head and said, 'I don't understand it at all. I'd certainly never have guessed the old dog was so sharp of hearing.'

But Susan replied, 'Didn't I always tell you our old dog was a wonderful watchdog? – but as usual, you thought you knew best.'

So everyone was happy again. The cat curled up by the stove. The dog lay down in his special place in the corner. And the fox had eaten so many sausages he could eat no more.

This story by the Brothers Grimm is retold by Mark Cohen.

The Prince and the Tortoise

A tale is told of a monarch, in the far-off ages of time, who had three sons: Ali, Husain and Muhammed. All were princely to look upon, valiant in war, skilled in the arts of peace; but the youngest was the most handsome, most brave and most good-hearted of the three. Their father loved them all, not favouring one more than the other, and secretly planned to leave to each an equal share of his kingdom and his wealth.

A time came when the boys were old enough for marriage, but since they had made no move to seek brides, the king called his wazir to him and asked for his advice.

The wazir, a man both wise and prudent, sat for an hour in thought, then said, 'O king of the centuries, what can avail against the finger of Destiny? Therefore I suggest this plan. Bid the three princes come to the terrace of the palace, each with bows and arrows; then, blindfolded with a cloth, each in turn must shoot an arrow high into the air. The house on which it falls will surely hold a daughter or other damsel. The owner of the house will then be visited and a marriage arranged. This will indeed be the work of Destiny.'

'Excellent counsel!' said the king. 'All this shall be done without delay.' And as soon as the boys returned from hunting, they were told to present themselves, equipped with bow and arrows, at the appointed place. First the oldest, Prince Ali, had a scarf tied over his eyes; he was turned round and round, then given the word to shoot. His arrow flew through the air and fell on the dwelling of a noble lord with a ripe young daughter. The second prince's arrow alighted on the walls of a fine mansion, the house of the king's commander-in-chief. He too had a girl who had reached the age for marriage. But the arrow of young Muhammed fell on a villa standing apart in a strange district, unknown to anyone in the palace. Messengers sent to investigate found no human inhabitant within, only a large and lonely tortoise.

Clearly chance had played a trick, and the prince was told to shoot again. For a second time he was blindfolded and turned about and about. Once more his arrow fell on the house of the lonely tortoise.

The king was enraged, and shouted to his son, 'You may have one more try. Call on the name of Allah, then send forth your arrow once again.'

Muhammed did as he was bid – and for the third time the arrow neatly alighted on the home of the tortoise, exactly as before.

'If the hand of Destiny shows in this,' murmured the king, 'it must intend the boy to remain a bachelor.' Aloud, he said, 'My son, this tortoise is not of our race nor of our religion; indeed, I do not recall a single case of a satisfactory union of one such with our kind. Surely it is Allah's will that you withdraw yourself from any thought of marrying.'

But the prince replied, 'O most mighty father, I read this differently. Destiny has appointed this tortoise to be my marriage partner, and marry her I must and shall.'

'Your interpretation may be right,' said the king, 'but in practice the notion is not only absurd – it is monstrous. How can you enter into marriage with a tortoise? I cannot understand your passion for the creature.'

'Do not mistake me,' said the young man. 'I have no great partiality for tortoises in general; indeed, I have hitherto given them little thought. It is this particular one that I wish to marry.'

Since further objection seemed useless and tiring, and since the king was fond of his son, he shrugged his shoulders, made no more protests, and gave orders for three great wedding feasts. The first two were held with widespread celebrations. But the third was a different matter; not a single guest attended, not even the other brothers and their wives, nor any court officials. Indeed, poor Prince Muhammed was mocked and scorned by all. Sneering smiles or averted faces everywhere met his gaze. And yet – though none but Allah could tell how he and the tortoise lived their lives together – the prince seemed well content with the ways of Destiny.

But the king, already weighed down by years and the burdens of state, and over-wearied by all

the recent events, began to pine and dwindle; he
ceased to eat; his eyesight failed; a shadow of his
former self, he lay awaiting death. The three sons
were much concerned; after consulting together,
they went to their father's bedside, where the eldest
spoke for the three.

'Dear father, we all desire to see you restored
to health, and so we bring you a plan. From
now on our wives will prepare whatever you eat.
They will do their utmost to revive your appetite
with enticing dishes, carefully cooked, and your
strength, and the sight of your eyes will soon
return.'

The king was greatly moved. 'But will not this
be an unwanted toil and labour to your wives?' he
asked.

At once the prince replied, 'Are not our wives
your slaves? Is there a better way for them to spend
their time? Noble father, it has been agreed between
us that, for a start, each shall prepare a dish, and you
will say which you find the most tempting, most
reviving, most delightful.'

'All is for the best,' said the father, and he
lay back, weak but hopeful, to await the savoury
fare.

So each wife set to work, the large and lonely tortoise no less than the other two. Smiling
to herself, she sent a confidential servant to her
older sister-in-law, begging her to send back any

mouse and rat droppings she could spare, as these had special value as seasoning.

The wife of Ali thought to herself, 'If this is so, I shall need all I have for my own use. Let her find her own.' Aloud, she said, 'Tell your mistress that I cannot give her what she requires as I have scarcely enough for myself.'

When this answer was brought to her, the tortoise laughed and laughed, then sent to the second sister-in-law, the wife of Husain, asking if she might have all spare hen and pigeon droppings for the special dish that she was preparing.

A sour refusal came from the woman, who was thinking to herself, 'There must be some rare merit in these things; I certainly will not give any of mine to that creature!'

The tortoise was so overcome with mirth when the servant brought back the message that she almost fell over; but she recovered herself and began to cook the dish that she really intended to bring to the sick monarch. At last it was done. She put it in a wicker basket, covered it with a rose-scented linen cloth, and told her servant to carry it carefully to the palace, where the offerings of the other wives were also being brought.

And now came the test. First, the dish of Prince Ali's wife was put before the king. He lifted the lid, expecting a delicious experience. But so foul an odour rose from the bowl that he fell into a swoon and had to be roused with fans and scented water. Presently he felt recovered enough to try the dish of the second daughter-in-law. He raised a spoonful to his lips – but so unpleasant and burning was the taste that he threw down the spoon, crying out to the anxious sons, 'What have I done to your wives that they should wish to kill me with their messes? Away, all of you!'

The young Muhammed now stepped forward, and begged his father to try the third dish, which he was certain would make up for both the other failures. The old king angrily refused. Then the prince knelt down and swore to eat the entire dish himself if the king did not care for it.

'At least, dear father, lift the cover.'

So the king signed to a slave to remove the cloth, murmuring as he did so, 'May Allah protect me!' But the odour which swirled towards him was so exquisite, so enticing and so savoury that it nourished the king before he lifted a morsel to his lips. His eyes began to clear; he ate the entire vesselful without stopping, then rounded it off with an excellent sherbet drink compounded of musk and snow. Finally he gave thanks to Allah, and called his son Muhammed to him, full of praise for the cooking of his wife.

'It is not her only talent, dear father,' said the prince. 'She has many gifts that would give you pleasure. Meanwhile she would rejoice to have

the privilege of preparing your food each day.'
The king agreed, and to celebrate his recovery
announced a banquet, especially for his three sons
and their wives.

At once the daughters-in-law began to make
their plans, wishing to appear at their best before
their father-in-law. The tortoise too gave careful
thought to the matter. First, she sent her special
servant to the older wife, asking if she would lend
the great goose in her courtyard as a steed for her
to ride to the palace.

The foolish woman refused, for the same jealous
reasoning as before – 'If she wants it, I'd do better
to use it myself.'

When the answer came, the tortoise laughed
and laughed, then sent the servant to the other
sister-in-law, asking for a loan of the he-goat in
her yard, for she wished to arrive in style at the
ceremony. Again the request was refused; again
the tortoise was overcome with mirth. What were
her own real plans? We shall know when we shall
know.

And now came the hour of the feast. The old king
and his queen awaited the arrival of the royal brides.
Suddenly a monstrous thing seemed to be moving
towards them – a huge goose was waddling along in
a cloud of dust, flapping and squawking under the
heavy burden of the first princess in the kingdom.
Following closely was a he-goat carrying the

second princess; she was desperately clutching the neck of the furious creature as it leapt and bleated under the load. Both women were covered with dust and dirt; their handsome gauzy clothes were torn to rags.

The king and queen watched aghast as the bedraggled, gibbering pair arrived, trying in vain to keep a steady seat on their frightened steeds. Words seemed to fail the monarch, but his mounting anger clearly showed in his face. At that moment messengers announced the coming of the third daughter-in-law. The king threw up his hands.

'If two humans can behave in this disgusting

111

fashion, what can we expect from a tortoise? Strange indeed are the ways of Allah!' But, even as he spoke, a glittering palanquin was carried into the hall, borne by four handsome attendants, richly dressed. Out of it stepped an unknown princess, lovely as the moon, in robes of exquisite beauty. All were amazed as Muhammed stepped forward and greeted her as his bride.

The transformation lightened the heart of the king; he ordered all to be seated, and the banquet to begin. The first course, as always, was a great dish of rice in butter. Before anyone could start, the fair princess raised the dish and poured its contents over her hair. At once each grain became a priceless pearl, adorning the damsel's tresses and running in a bright and tinkling torrent to the floor. While the company gazed, open-mouthed at this marvel, the princess seized a large tureen full of thick green soup and poured this also over her head. The green drops became a sea of emeralds, mingling in ravishing fashion with the pearls in her hair, the overflow forming brilliant pools on the floor.

The king was quite delighted. Then the servants brought fresh supplies, and the feast was about to start. But the two other wives, gnawed with jealousy, could not bear to be outdone. The older grasped the new dish of rice, the other the tureen of soup, and they poured them over their heads. But the result for each was a horrible mess, sickening to behold. The king was altogether disgusted with the women; he banished them from the feast and from the palace, saying that he never wished to hear of them again. Their husbands led them away, and that was that. But the Prince Muhammed and his magical bride remained, for they pleased the heart of the king.

First, the monarch embraced them, saying, 'From this day, my palace is your home, your home my palace.' Then he wrote a will, making his youngest son the heir to his throne and kingdom.

The princess now sent her servant to fetch the large and lonely shell, and she burnt it, there and then, for she did not wish to vex her old father-in-law by appearing in it thereafter. Many were the children of Muhammed and the princess in the years to come; happy were their lives throughout. Wonderful are the ways of Allah!

This story is a retelling of Naomi Lewis of the traditional Arabian Nights tale.

Nothing to be Afraid of

'Robin won't give you any trouble,' said Auntie Lynn. 'He's very quiet.'

Anthea knew how quiet Robin was. At present he was sitting under the table and, until Auntie Lynn mentioned his name, she had forgotten that he was there.

Auntie Lynn put a carrier bag on the armchair.

'There's plenty of clothes, so you won't need to do any washing, and there's a spare pair of pyjamas in case – well, you know. In case . . .'

'Yes,' said Mum, firmly. 'He'll be all right. I'll ring you tonight and let you know how he's getting along.' She looked at the clock. 'Now, hadn't *you* better be getting along?'

She saw Auntie Lynn to the front door and Anthea heard them saying goodbye to each other. Mum almost told Auntie Lynn to stop worrying and have a good time, which would have been a mistake because Auntie Lynn was going up North to a funeral.

Auntie Lynn was not really an Aunt, but she had once been at school with Anthea's mum, and she was the kind of person who couldn't manage without a handle to her name; so Robin was not Anthea's cousin. Robin was not anything much, except four years old, and he looked a lot younger; probably because nothing ever happened to him. Auntie Lynn kept no pets that might give Robin germs, and never bought him toys that had sharp corners to dent him or wheels that could be swallowed. He wore balaclava helmets and bobble hats in winter to protect his tender ears, and a knitted vest under his shirt in summer in case he overheated himself and caught a chill from his own sweat.

'Perspiration,' said Auntie Lynn.

His face was as pale and flat as a saucer of milk, and his eyes floated in it like drops of cod-liver oil. This was not so surprising as he was full to the back teeth with cod-liver oil; also with extract of malt, concentrated orange juice and calves-foot jelly. When you picked him up you expected him to squelch, like a hot-water bottle full of half-set custard.

Anthea lifted the tablecloth and looked at him.

'Hello, Robin.'

Robin stared at her with his flat eyes and went back to sucking his woolly doggy that had flat eyes also, of sewn-on felt, because glass ones might find their way into Robin's appendix and cause damage. Anthea wondered how long it would be before he noticed that his mother had gone. Probably he wouldn't, any more than he would notice when she came back.

Mum closed the front door and joined Anthea in looking under the table at Robin. Robin's mouth turned down at the corners, and Anthea hoped he would cry so that they could cuddle him. It seemed impolite to cuddle him before he needed it. Anthea was afraid to go any closer.

'What a little troll,' said Mum, sadly, lowering the tablecloth. 'I suppose he'll come out when he's hungry.'

Anthea doubted it.

*

Robin didn't want any lunch or any tea.

'Do you think he's pining?' said Mum. Anthea did not. Anthea had a nasty suspicion that he was like this all the time. He went to bed without making a fuss and fell asleep before the light was out, as if he were too bored to stay awake. Anthea left her bedroom door open, hoping that he would have a nightmare so that she could go in and comfort him, but Robin slept all night without a squeak, and woke in the morning as flat-faced as before. Wall-eyed Doggy looked more excitable than Robin did.

'If only we had a proper garden,' said Mum, as Robin went under the table again, leaving his breakfast eggs scattered round the plate. 'He might run about.'

Anthea thought that this was unlikely, and in any case they didn't have a proper garden, only a yard at the back and a stony strip in front, without a fence.

'Can I take him to the park?' said Anthea.

Mum looked doubtful. 'Do you think he wants to go?'

'No,' said Anthea, peering under the tablecloth. 'I don't think he wants to do anything, but he can't sit there all day.'

'I bet he can,' said Mum. 'Still, I don't think he should. All right, take him to the park, but keep

quiet about it. I don't suppose Lynn thinks you're
safe in traffic.'

'He might tell her.'

'Can he talk?'

Robin, still clutching wall-eyed Doggy, plodded
beside her all the way to the park, without once
trying to jam his head between the library railings
or get run over by a bus.

'Hold my hand, Robin,' Anthea said as they left
the house, and he clung to her like a lamprey.

The park was not really a park at all; it was a
garden. It did not even pretend to be a park and
the notice by the gate said KING STREET GARDENS,
in case anyone tried to use it as a park. The grass
was as green and as flat as the front-room carpet,
but the front-room carpet had a path worn across it
from the door to the fireplace, and here there were
more notices that said KEEP OFF THE GRASS, so
that the gritty white paths went obediently round
the edge, under the orderly trees that stood in a
row like the queue outside a fish shop. There were
bushes in each corner and one shelter with a bench
in it. Here and there brown holes in the grass, full
of raked earth, waited for next year's flowers, but
there were no flowers now, and the bench had been
taken out of the shelter because the shelter was supposed to be a summer-house, and you couldn't have
people using a summer-house in winter.

Robin stood by the gates and gaped, with Doggy depending limply from his mouth where he held it by one ear, between his teeth. Anthea decided that if they met anyone she knew, she would explain that Robin was only two, but very big for his age.

'Do you want to run, Robin?'

Robin shook his head.

'There's nothing to be afraid of. You can go all the way round, if you like, but you mustn't walk on the grass or pick things.'

Robin nodded. It was the kind of place that he understood.

Anthea sighed. 'Well, let's walk round, then.'

They set off. At each corner, where the bushes were, the path diverged. One part went in front of the bushes, one part round the back of them. On the first circuit Robin stumped glumly beside Anthea in front of the bushes. The second time round she felt a very faint tug at her hand. Robin wanted to go his own way.

This called for a celebration. Robin could think. Anthea crouched down on the path until they were at the same level.

'You want to walk round the back of the bushes, Robin?'

'Yiss,' said Robin.

Robin could *talk*.

'All right, but listen.' She lowered her voice to a whisper. 'You must be very careful. That path is called Leopard Walk. Do you know what a leopard is?'

'Yiss.'

'There are two leopards down there. They live in the bushes. One is a good leopard and the other's a bad leopard. The good leopard has black spots. The bad leopard has red spots. If you see the bad leopard you must say, "Die leopard die or I'll kick you in the eye," and run like anything. Do you understand?'

Robin tugged again.

'Oh no,' said Anthea. 'I'm going *this* way. If you want to go down Leopard Walk, you'll have to go on your own. I'll meet you at the other end. Remember, if it's got red spots, run like mad.'

Robin trotted away. The bushes were just high enough to hide him, but Anthea could see the bobble on his hat doddering along. Suddenly the bobble gathered speed and Anthea had to run to reach the end of the bushes first.

'Did you see the bad leopard?'

'No,' said Robin, but he didn't look too sure.

'Why were you running, then?'

'I just wanted to.'

'You've dropped Doggy,' said Anthea. Doggy lay on the path with his legs in the air, halfway down Leopard Walk.

'You get him,' said Robin.

'No, *you* get him,' said Anthea. 'I'll wait here.'

Robin moved off, reluctantly. She waited until he had recovered Doggy and then shouted, 'I can see the bad leopard in the bushes!' Robin raced back to safety. 'Did you say, "Die leopard die or I'll kick you in the eye"?' Anthea demanded.

'No,' Robin said guiltily.

'Then he'll *kill* us,' said Anthea. 'Come on, run. We've got to get to that tree. He can't hurt us once we're under that tree.'

They stopped running under the twisted boughs of a weeping ash. 'This is a python tree,' said Anthea. 'Look, you can see the python wound round the trunk.'

'What's a python?' said Robin, backing off.

'Oh, it's just a great big snake that squeezes people to death,' said Anthea. 'A python could

easily eat a leopard. That's why leopards won't walk under this tree, you see, Robin.'

Robin looked up. 'Could it eat us?'

'Yes, but it won't if we walk on our heels.' They walked on their heels to the next corner.

'Are there leopards down there?'

'No, but we must never go down there anyway. That's Poison Alley. All the trees are poisonous. They drip poison. If one bit of poison fell on your head, you'd die.'

'I've got my hat on,' said Robin, touching the bobble to make sure.

'It would burn right through your hat,' Anthea assured him. 'Right into your brains. *Fzzzzzzz*.'

They by-passed Poison Alley and walked on over the manhole cover that clanked.

'What's that?'

'That's the Fever Pit. If anyone lifts that manhole cover, they get a terrible disease. There's this terrible disease down there, Robin, and if the lid comes off, the disease will get out and people will die. I should think there's enough disease down there to kill everybody in this town. It's ever so loose, look.'

'Don't lift it! Don't lift it!' Robin screamed, and ran to the shelter for safety.

'Don't go in there,' yelled Anthea. 'That's where the Greasy Witch lives.' Robin bounced out of the shelter as though he were on elastic.

'Where's the Greasy Witch?'

'Oh, you can't see her,' said Anthea, 'but you can tell where she is because she smells so horrible. I think she must be somewhere about. Can't you smell her now?'

Robin sniffed the air and clasped Doggy more tightly.

'And she leaves oily marks wherever she goes. Look, you can see them on the wall.'

Robin looked at the wall. Someone had been very busy, if not the Greasy Witch. Anthea was glad on the whole that Robin could not read.

'The smell's getting worse, isn't it, Robin? I think we'd better go down here and then she won't find us.'

'She'll see us.'

'No, she won't. She can't see with her eyes because they're full of grease. She sees with her ears, but I expect they're all waxy. She's a filthy old witch, really.'

They slipped down a secret-looking path that went round the back of the shelter.

'Is the Greasy Witch down here?' said Robin, fearfully.

'I don't know,' said Anthea. 'Let's investigate.' They tiptoed round the side of the shelter. The path was damp and slippery. 'Filthy old witch. She's certainly *been* here,' said Anthea. 'I think she's gone now. I'll just have a look.'

She craned her neck round the corner of the

shelter. There was a sort of glade in the bushes, and in the middle was a stand-pipe, with a tap on top. The pipe was lagged with canvas, like a scaly skin.

'Frightful Corner,' said Anthea. Robin put his cautious head round the edge of the shelter.

'What's that?'

Anthea wondered if it could be a dragon, up on the tip of its tail and ready to strike, but on the other side of the bushes was the brick back wall of the King Street Public Conveniences, and at that moment she heard the unmistakable sound of a cistern flushing.

'It's a Lavatory Demon,' she said. 'Quick! We've got to get away before the water stops, or he'll have us.'

They ran all the way to the gates, where they could see the church clock, and it was almost time for lunch.

Auntie Lynn fetched Robin home next morning, and three days later she was back again, striding up the path like a warrior queen going into battle, with Robin dangling from her hand, and Doggy dangling from Robin's hand.

Mum took her into the front room, closing the door. Anthea sat on the stairs and listened. Auntie Lynn was in full throat and furious, so it was easy enough to hear what she had to say.

'I want a word with that young lady,' said Auntie Lynn. 'And I want to know what she's been telling him.' Her voice dropped, and Anthea could hear only certain fateful words: 'Leopards . . . poison trees . . . snakes . . . diseases!'

Mum said something very quietly that Anthea did not hear, and then Auntie Lynn turned up the volume once more.

'Won't go to bed unless I leave the door open . . . wants the light on . . . up and down to him all night . . . won't go to the bathroom on his own. He says the – the —' she hesitated, 'the *toilet* demons will get him. He nearly broke his neck running downstairs this morning.'

Mum spoke again, but Auntie Lynn cut in like a band-saw.

'Frightened out of his wits! He follows me every-where.'

The door opened slightly, and Anthea got ready to bolt, but it was Robin who came out, with his thumb in his mouth and circles round his eyes. Under his arm was soggy Doggy, ears chewed to nervous rags.

Robin looked up at Anthea through the banisters.

'Let's go to the park,' he said.

This story is by Jan Mark.

Lucott the Pirate

Lucott was a pirate and he wasn't one of the dashing golden-hearted kind, either. He was black-browed and black-bearded and he had a black temper to match. He and his crew harried the Somerset coast with the skull and crossbones flying and many a prisoner walked the frisky plank when Black Lucott's men were hunting. He had gold by the sackful, taken from rich merchantmen and he hoarded it in a chest in Porlock harbour. The people of Porlock spoke softly to him when he came ashore, because of his treasure and his men's sharp cutlasses, but there wasn't a soul in the port who didn't breathe a sigh of relief when they saw him leave harbour and put to sea again.

Well, years went by and Lucott grew crueller and fiercer with every one that passed. There were plenty of brave men tried to put a stop to him but he had a good ship and a well-trained crew and he always got away scot free. But he met his match at last in a French privateer. He fought it out from morning till night, broadside to broadside with all guns blazing, but at the end of the day, Lucott's vessel sank to the bottom of the sea and every hand went with her.

When the people of Porlock learnt that Lucott was dead they were pleased and relieved. They held a service to settle his soul and then they shared out his treasure and thought they'd heard the last of him. But they were out of luck.

Next morning the Sunday bells rang out and everybody in Porlock put on gloves and hats and set off for church. All went well until the parson mounted the steps to the pulpit to give the sermon. Then, all of a sudden, there was a sound like a thunderclap as the door burst open. A huge, black-bearded figure came stamping up to the altar. Lucott had returned from the dead.

There was pandemonium in the church. Children were shrieking, young ladies fainting, and the butcher's wife fell into hysterics. The parson hammered on the pulpit till his hands were sore but all to no purpose. It was the organist who saved the day. He played such a mighty chord that the uproar was drowned and the church fell silent.

The parson glared at Lucott and pointed a shaking finger.

'Out!' he said. 'This is no place for you.'

But Lucott threw back his head and laughed.

'Why not?' he asked dangerously. 'If I've a fancy to come to church, you can't stop me.'

With that he strolled over to the front pew and settled himself comfortably.

'Carry on!' he said. 'Don't mind me. I like a bit of preaching.'

So the parson gathered his wits together and went on. But it was a poor sort of sermon he gave and the last hymn was a disgrace. Nobody could hit their top notes with Lucott sitting there. They gave it up as a bad job and scrapped the last verse altogether. And after the parson gave the blessing, you couldn't see them for dust. Mrs Wilkin's hat was squashed flat as a pancake in the scrimmage and even the vicar was reeling.

'You'll have to lay him, sir,' said the people's warden. 'We can't go through that again.'

But the parson looked doubtful. 'I don't know how!' he protested. 'What if he won't go?'

'You must make him. Show him who's master.'

The parson shook his head. 'Not without help. Find me eleven other clergymen and I'll have a go, but do it on my own I will not. It's asking too much.'

Everyone agreed that was fair and next day the church wardens set out to look for eleven more parsons. It wasn't easy. News of Lucott's ghost had already spread and word was out that he'd be a hard soul to lay.

'I doubt if I can help,' said the vicar of Crowcombe politely. 'I've not got a lot of experience of this type of work. And they say Oxford men are best anyway. I'm Cambridge myself.'

'I'm too old for the job,' mumbled old Canon Truebody from Wells. 'You need strong young fellers who ain't afraid of a scrap.'

'Too busy,' said the new curate of Porlock Weir. 'Try Glastonbury.'

They did try Glastonbury. They tried every parish in Somerset. They scoured the whole country-side and at that they had a job to muster twelve. But one cold morning in February, a dozen pale and nervous clergymen gathered outside Porlock church. Each carried a Bible and a candle and they all looked as if they'd very much rather be elsewhere.

'Come on,' said the archdeacon of Bristol, squaring his shoulders. 'Let's get it over.'

He marched into the church, gripping his candle so tight it squashed out of shape. The others shuffled after him, their footsteps echoing on the stone floor. One or two lingered on the threshold.

'Lucott!' shouted the archdeacon. 'Show yourself!'

Eerie laughter rang round the church, but the ghost did not appear. The clergymen felt a cold wind whipping their robes and the candles flickered madly.

'Lucott!' cried the archdeacon again. 'Come out!'

There was a bloodcurdling shriek and all the candles went out. The church bells rang wildly and then, just as suddenly, fell silent.

'For the last time, Lucott, are you coming or not?'

'I am coming!' called a tremendous voice, and with a swoop a vast shadow was upon them – a shadow so cold that its very touch chilled them.

It was too much. The archdeacon stood his ground, but even he couldn't steady his companions. Someone broke away, dropping book and candle in a rush to escape. Suddenly it was a rout. Everyone was caught up in the panic and within seconds only the ghost remained within Porlock Church.

The villagers were very dashed when they heard what had happened.

'Seems to me it's a parson's job!' said some. 'If they won't take him on, who will?'

But then, as the blacksmith pointed out, it was one thing to talk about ghost laying, and quite another to do it – especially when the ghost was Black Lucott. So they thanked the clergymen kindly for their trouble and thought none the worse of them.

But the story went round and, by and by, the vicar of Watchet got wind of it. He was a hard-riding, drinking sort of parson and he'd missed his chance at Lucott because it was a hunting day. When he heard the story he was furious.

'Impudence!' he said. 'Sheer insolence. I'll teach that ghost manners.'

He called all the clergymen together and gave them a tremendous talking to.

'You're letting him think he's won,' he said. 'But we'll show him better. I want the whole pack of you up at the church tomorrow and we'll see who chases who out of it.'

'But you don't understand,' said the young curate of West Zoyland nervously. 'He really is very powerful. Quite frankly, I wouldn't care to face him again.'

'Very well,' said the vicar of Watchet. 'Then I'll go in on my own and the rest of you can follow later. But I'll expect you outside the church at nine o'clock sharp.'

Well, the vicar of Watchet had a fierce way of looking at you and somehow none of the other clergymen cared to argue. So at nine o'clock on the dot they came together, books and candles at the ready.

'Right,' said the vicar. 'You wait here. If I'm not out by ten you're to come in and get me.'

They nodded nervously and watched him enter.

At first they could only hear his voice, calling loudly and impatiently for the ghost.

'I do wish he'd be careful,' murmured the curate of West Zoyland. 'Lucott isn't a hunt servant, after all.'

And indeed it did sound as if the ghost had taken offence for all of a sudden there came such a screech that their hair stood on end. But as it died away, they heard the vicar's voice, rising to a roar.

'Will you hold your tongue! And stop flapping that cloak about *at once*!'

His voice dropped to a mumble and there was no more from the ghost. After a little while, some of the bolder sort crept closer. But they still couldn't hear properly so they jumped up and peered through one of the stained glass windows to find out what was going on.

The scene took their breath away. There was the vicar of Watchet, thumbs in waistcoat pockets, holding forth like the village schoolmaster. And there was the ghost, slumped down in a pew, scowling, mutinous, but quiet. The vicar seemed to be putting it through an examination.

'Now . . . ' came his voice clearly. 'Answer me this. How many angels can stand on the head of a pin?'

Lucott's face twisted with the effort of thought. His great fists clenched and he flushed scarlet.

'How would I know?' he muttered at last. 'Let me be.'

'Oh no,' cried the vicar. 'If you can't answer, you're in my power. That's the rule. You there!' he called to one of the watchers. 'Fetch me a donkey as quick as you can. We've got him now.'

So somebody ran off to find a donkey while Lucott's ghost and the Watchet vicar glared at each other. When it arrived, the vicar said sharply, 'Get on it, Lucott, and be quick about it.'

'Not I!' said Lucott. 'A flea-bitten little neddy! I want a horse.'

'Well, you're not getting one. You failed my question so now you must do as you're told. You'll get on that donkey and you'll ride to Watchet with me.'

For one long minute it looked as if Lucott would rebel. The watching parsons held their breath and the vicar of Watchet stood like a statue. Then Lucott broke. With a snarl of rage he mounted the donkey and off they went.

All the way to Watchet they rode, with Lucott grumbling at every step. The vicar said in a low voice, 'He's in an ugly mood. Someone had better go ahead to warn everyone to keep clear. I don't want anybody on the street when he arrives.'

The people of Watchet needed no persuading. By the time the party got there, every street was deserted, and every door closed. Little children had been snatched inside and the shopkeepers had shuttered their windows. There wasn't a soul to be seen.

But one man hadn't listened to the warning. Tom Paxton, the biggest gossip in Somerset, was waiting in hiding behind the rocks on the seashore. He hadn't bothered to get indoors, because he always thought he knew best, and now he was waiting for a glimpse of the famous Porlock ghost.

Down the silent streets rode the vicar, with the donkey shambling behind him. When they reached the seashore, the vicar raised his arms, ready to return Lucott to the depths. But just as he did so, the old pirate spotted Paxton.

'Avast there! A spy! I'll teach you to pry into my affairs if it's the last thing I do!'

Before the vicar could stop him, he swept down on Paxton and struck him such a blow he fell senseless. He was bending to finish his work when the vicar called out in a voice like thunder.

'Down!' he cried. 'Down to the bottom of the sea and never come back again.'

And down Lucott went, as if that last rebellion had worn him out. There was a cry, a great splash and that was the end of him. The vicar went back to Watchet and the Porlock people took up their affairs again. But they didn't forget Lucott. They never have. And to this day, if you go to Porlock, they'll tell you the tale of the laying of the pirate's ghost.

This story is by Dinah Starkey.

Stone

With his box on his back Sly trudged into the village. A hog-hole he saw at once, a couple of dozen rubbishy little hovels round a church no better than a barn. Lucky to pick up fourpence

here, but a man must work his trade and take what he can get, or he'll lose his self-respect, and that's all that matters, isn't it?

One of the hovels was trying to pretend it was an inn. That is to say it had a branch of dead broom lashed to the doorpost. Sly went into the dark little room, put his box down where it would be noticed, bought himself a small mug of cider and a hunk of black bread, and waited for his customers to come in from the fields.

They came. Without seeming to look at them he reckoned them up – four Bumpkins, two Hicks and a Clod. They stared at the stranger, and even longer at his box, which was a three-foot cube, bright-painted with stars and signs, and had air-holes in the top. Occasional scratching noises came from inside it, and once a strange mewing hiss. (Sly had a trick of casting his voice.) He sat relaxed. No need to get into conversation, start up a patter – one of them would ask in a moment, one of the Hicks. Hicks always liked to get their word in . . .

'What've you got in your box, then?'

'Cockatrice,' said Sly in a bored voice.

'Cockawhat?' said the Clod.

'Never met a cockatrice?' said Sly. 'Well of course you haven't, or you wouldn't be here, in this charming little village of yours. Instead there'd be a fine stone statue of you in the place where you met the cockatrice.'

'Give us a look, then,' said the Clod, hog-eager. Sly sighed.

'Don't you listen?' he asked. 'You *can't* look at a cockatrice. If you look at him at the same moment he looks at you, and your eyes meet . . .'

He snapped a bony finger and let the sound die in their ears.

'. . . you turn to stone,' he whispered.

'Gor!' said the Clod.

'Cold, hard stone, never to move again,' said Sly.

They thought about it. Sly sensed their slow minds grinding. He made the mewing noise come from the box. The Hick who had first spoken stared at him, then quickly away.

'What's your cockatrice look like then?' he asked the air in front of him. Quite quick, for a Hick, thought Sly.

'Well, he's mostly a sort of brassy colour,' he said. 'Silver stripes along his back. The front of him's a bantam cock, far as the legs, but all behind there his tail end's more a big lizard. If you were fool enough to look at him once, you'd look at him twice.'

'You seen him, then?' asked the Hick, still to the air.

'You could say so,' said Sly.

'Why you not turned to stone then?' shouted the Hick.

The Bumpkins and the other Hick banged their

table and yelled with triumph at the cleverness of their companion. Even the Clod got it in the end. Sly smiled at the uproar and pulled from his belt-purse a square of polished yellow metal which he breathed on and rubbed on his sleeve. Then he twisted away and held the thing up so that he could see the men's reflection.

'You could say I am seeing you, my friends,' he said. 'I say I am not. All I am seeing is your image. That is how I know what a cockatrice looks like.'

They argued the point among themselves till the next thought struck them.

'Give us a look, then,' pleaded a Bumpkin. 'Give us a look in your bit of brass.'

And they came crowding round, hooked. Sly resisted – the cockatrice was not for show. He was taking it to the Emperor of Tartary, who needed it for the execution of criminals since his religion did not allow him to shed blood. What would happen to the village, to the whole countryside, if it got loose? Why, he took his own life in his hands each time he opened the lid to feed the monster. And so on.

Twenty minutes later he was out in the road with the whole village – Bumpkins, Wenches, Hags, Clods, Besoms, Hicks, the lot – crowding round, each eager to pay their farthing and take their peep in the brass mirror. The mirror, it has to be said, was not very good. The metal was well polished but there was a slight ripple on it which made the reflection waver. Still, if you looked carefully you certainly saw something moving in the depths of the box, with a front end like a bantam and a back end not like any bird that ever was born. All the time the horrible mewing hiss came from the box, and Sly would listen and suddenly snatch the lid and cram it down and say the creature was restless and might try to flap out and then they would all be stone. That added to the excitement.

Half of them had had their peep when Sly sensed a change, a hush at the edge of the crowd. He put the lid on the box and turned, smiling. The crowd parted respectfully, and he saw there was no need to worry. It was only a Dotard, leaning on the shoulder of a Clodling. A dotard of Dotards, snow-white beard, eyes deep under shagged brows – the village priest, no doubt, but a Dotard for all that.

'What is happening?' he quavered.

The whole crowd tried to tell him at once. He came doddering through, leaning on the Clodling's shoulder. Sly started into his patter. The Dotard listened, nodding and wheezing, and listened again with his head cocked to one side when the mewing noise came, sudden and loud, from the box. He groped and found a farthing. The crowd whispered among themselves as Sly pushed the old fool into place and positioned the mirror.

Sly inched the lid up. Suddenly the Dotard straightened from his crouch. He had both hands on the rim of the box. For all his age he was stronger and quicker than Sly had guessed. He wrenched the box away and tipped it right over.

'Don't look! Don't look!' yelled Sly.

But already most of the village had seen an out-raged bantam-cock running across the mud road. Fastened over its tail-feathers was a leather exten-sion painted with scales.

Sitting on a sun-baked rock Sly stared back over the plain. Behind him bare foothills rose towards mountains. He brooded. There was one particular village in that plain, three days' journey away now, but here at this moment in his thoughts . . . of course he had been caught out before, jeered at and pelted before, had his takings seized back before, but for it to happen there! Clods, Bumpkins, Hicks and a Dotard! If you'd lumped the contents of their skulls together they wouldn't have added up to one brain . . . He could get another bantam, make another lizard tail – no need for a new box, as they'd thrust the old one over his head when they pushed him out of the village . . . but their jeering! There'd been a note in it, as though they thought it was Sly who was the Clod . . . something they knew and he didn't, something about the Dotard . . . Well, one day Sly would come back and teach them a lesson. A man has to keep his self-respect. That's all that matters, isn't it?

Just below where he sat the sun's heat bounced back from a flat rock. Beyond that the slope dropped away out of sight. He heard a sudden chirruping shriek, a small animal in terror. A mouse raced up on to the rock with a weasel looping behind it. Instead of pouncing at once the weasel overtook the mouse, heading it off and driving it back shrieking over the rock. Sly did not interfere. If the weasel chose to torment its prey before killing it that was none of his business; in fact it fitted his thoughts about Bumpkin village to watch the game played out.

But that did not happen. As the mouse came skittering back on a new line it suddenly froze still. The weasel froze too. Six inches in front of the mouse the surface of the rock had moved, had risen and become a large, squat lizard, the exact colour of the rock. Sluggishly, on splayed legs, it waddled forward and ate the mouse in a single gulp. It raised its head towards the weasel, which arched its back and spat. Out of the lizard's spine rose a bright purple fin. The weasel's brown and white fur turned grey. It did not move again. It was stone.

Still with its tail towards Sly, the lizard lowered the fin and sank down on to the rock. So exactly did its colour match the surface that it seemed to vanish, but with the stone weasel to guide him Sly could just make out where it lay.

He sat still, shaking with terror and thrill, and then nerving himself to move. When he did so it was with a thief's caution. First he undid the hinge-lacings of his box and laid the lid aside. Then he rose and carrying the box bottom up crept down the slope, step by slow step, not daring to dislodge one pebble. All the time he watched the surface of the rock in front of the weasel. His neck-muscles ached with tension, ready to jerk his head aside at the slightest movement. Only as he banged the box down did the lizard stir, and then it was too late.

Sly weighted the box with a boulder and scrambled back for the lid. He slid it probingly under until he felt the lizard scrabble against it. Firmly he slid the box towards him, forcing the lizard up on to the lid, until he had box and lid fitted together. He put his hand under the lid, closed his eyes, and turned the box over, keeping the lid closed tight as he did so. With a sigh of relief he heard the lizard flop first against the side then down on to the bottom. He weighted the lid down and paused, trembling.

The weasel caught his eye and he picked it up. It seemed to have been carved from a dark

146

stone, smooth and very heavy. It was perfect in every hair and claw. He fetched his pack and put it away.

Now he realized that he would need to open the lid in order to replace the lacings. He hesitated. The lizard had made no sound. At last, with his tongue flickering over his lips, he got out his brass mirror and polished it on his sleeve. He knelt by the box and inched the lid up, holding the mirror at the proper angle to show him the bottom. It was dim down there (as it was meant to be, so that Bumpkins should not see too clearly). He made out a dark shape on the wood of the bottom. It did not stir. He opened the lid further to let in more light.

Now the rippled image moved. The fin rose. Large eyes opened, gazing up. In the blurred depths of the brass the two sight-lines met, Sly's and the lizard's. Even like that, even so faintly encountered, Sly felt the icy shaft of the creature's gaze lance into his brain, into his soul.

The neck-muscles knew what to do. They jerked the head aside and he staggered back, letting the lid snap down. It took an hour for the sun to warm him through. He fastened the lacings by touch and made his way down the mountain.

Next morning he had a slice of luck. He met a merchant on the road and sold him the weasel for five silver coins, which meant that he'd have no need to earn his living as a mountebank for a good few days. The idea came to him that he might now be able to give up travelling and settle in a rich town where he could make his living as a dealer in statues. Dogs, cats, squirrels . . . people? Why, yes, if he could find a busy orphanage and make a deal with its warden . . . But before any of that there was the matter of Bumpkin Village.

Deliberately Sly waited till Sunday before he went back.

Everybody was in the little mud church, the people on their knees, the Dotard wheezing through the prayers. Sly waited in the porch for the last Amen.

He flung the door open, strode to the bottom of the aisle and put his box down.

'You wanted to see a real cockatrice,' he cried. 'Well, I have brought you one!'

Perhaps there was something in his voice that told them that this time he did not lie. They stayed where they stood, all but the Dotard, who came doddering down the aisle, leaning as always on his Clodling's shoulder.

'Well, well,' he wheezed, 'a cockatrice? A real one? I did not believe that such a thing could be. I would like to see that.'

Sly stood back and flung the lid up, keeping his

head turned well away. The priest came blundering up, so stupid-eager that he let go of the Clodling and almost blundered into the box. He put a trembling old hand on the edge. What if he turned it over as before? Sly tensed to dart away. He might lose his cockatrice, but he would have a church full of statues. Very striking some of them might be . . . *And* he would have his revenge . . .

The Dotard craned over the box.

'My friend,' he murmured, 'I think your cockatrice is dead.'

Sly took a pace forward, raising his arm to strike the old man in his fury and disappointment. As he did so he glanced down into the box.

The purple fin was raised, the pale eyes staring upwards, meeting Sly's glance. The ghastly shaft seared through brain, soul, body, and he was stone.

'Put the lid back,' said the priest. 'Do not look, anyone. Be careful.'

They did as he said, among whispers and mutters of shock. They waited for his next order. He would know what to do. He had been a scholar, a dweller in cities, adviser to kings, who had come back in old age to the village and people of his birth.

'Not a cockatrice, of course,' he said. 'There is no such animal – it is a fable. I think our unfortunate friend must have found a basilisk, but let us not grieve too much for him. He might have done greater harm if he had been allowed. Now I have read that there is only one safe method for dealing with a basilisk. Does anyone possess a good mirror?'

It happened that there was a woman who had just such a thing in her hut. Long ago she had been servant to a gentlewoman, who had given the useless luxury to her as a wedding-gift. She ran and brought it. They carried the box out into daylight. The priest made them all stand back while he opened the lid and then held the mirror flat over the box, so that it reflected straight down. He tilted it slightly this way and that, to make sure. Then he borrowed a crook from a shepherd and prodded around in the bottom of the box until he felt the tip scrape on stone. Satisfied, he turned the box over. A stone thing clattered out.

'Why,' said someone, ' 'tis nowt like a cock at all. 'Tis more of a great lizard.'

'A dragon, you mean,' said someone else.

'Yes, that's what it is,' said the Hick who had first spoken to Sly in the inn. He always liked to get his word in.

' 'Tis a dragon,' he said, 'and look, why, you'd only need to put some kind of spear in the fellow's grip where he's got his arm up and he'd do for St Michael, and then we'd have our own holy statue, like we've always wanted, St Michael killing the dragon.'

'St George, he was the one with the dragon,' said someone else.

The old priest smiled and nodded as they argued it out. They were good simple people. Then he reached out and felt for the shoulder of the boy he needed to lead him everywhere, and told him to take him home for his dinner.

This story is by Peter Dickinson.

Baba Yaga

Once upon a time there was a widowed old man who lived alone in a hut with his little daughter. Very merry they were together, and they used to smile at each other over a table just piled with bread and jam. Everything went well, until the old man took it into his head to marry again.

Yes, the old man became foolish in the years of his old age, and he took another wife. And so the poor little girl had a stepmother. And after that everything changed. There was no more bread and jam on the table, and no more playing bo-peep, first this side of the samovar and then that, as she sat with her father at tea. It was worse than that, for she never did sit at tea. The stepmother said that everything that went wrong was the little girl's fault. And the old man believed his new wife, and so there were no more kind words for his little daughter. Day after day the stepmother used to say that the little girl was too naughty to

153

sit at table. And then she would throw her a crust and tell her to get out of the hut and go and eat it somewhere else.

And the poor little girl used to go away by herself into the shed in the yard, and wet the dry crust with her tears, and eat it all alone. Ah me! she often wept for the old days, and she often wept at the thought of the days that were to come.

Mostly she wept because she was all alone, until one day she found a little friend in the shed. She was hunched up in a corner of the shed, eating her crust and crying bitterly, when she heard a little noise. It was like this: scratch – scratch. It was just that, a little grey mouse who lived in a hole.

Out he came, his little pointed nose and his long whiskers, his little round ears and his bright eyes. Out came his little humpy body and his long tail. And then he sat up on his hind legs, and curled his tail twice round himself and looked at the little girl.

The little girl, who had a kind heart, forgot all her sorrows, and took a scrap of her crust and threw it to the little mouse. The mouseykin nibbled and nibbled, and there, it was gone, and he was looking for another. She gave him another bit, and presently that was gone, and another and another, until there was no crust left for the little girl. Well, she didn't mind that. You see, she was so happy seeing the little mouse nibbling and nibbling.

When the crust was done the mouseykin looks up at her with his little bright eyes, and 'Thank you,' he says, in a little squeaky voice. 'Thank you,' he says; 'you are a kind little girl, and I am only a mouse, and I've eaten all your crust. But there is one thing I can do for you, and that is to tell you to take care. The old woman in the hut (and that was the cruel stepmother) is own sister to Baba Yaga, the bony-legged, the witch. So if ever she sends you on a message to your aunt, you come and tell me. For Baba Yaga would eat you soon enough with her iron teeth if you did not know what to do.'

'Oh, thank you,' said the little girl; and just then she heard the stepmother calling to her to come in and clean up the tea things, and tidy the house, and brush out the floor, and clean everybody's boots.

So off she had to go.

When she went in she had a good look at her stepmother, and sure enough she had a long nose, and she was as bony as a fish with all the flesh picked off, and the little girl thought of Baba Yaga and shivered, though she did not feel so bad when she remembered the mouseykin out there in the shed in the yard.

The very next morning it happened. The old man went off to pay a visit to some friends of his in the next village, just as I go off sometimes to see old Fedor, God be with him. And as soon as the old man was out of sight the wicked stepmother called the little girl.

'You are to go today to your dear little aunt in the forest,' says she, 'and ask her for a needle and thread to mend a shirt.'

'But here is a needle and thread,' says the little girl.

'Hold your tongue,' says the stepmother, and she gnashes her teeth, and they make a noise like clattering tongs. 'Hold your tongue,' she says. 'Didn't I tell you you are to go today to your dear little aunt to ask for a needle and thread to mend a shirt?'

'How shall I find her?' says the little girl, nearly

ready to cry, for she knew that her aunt was Baba Yaga, the bony-legged, the witch.

The stepmother took hold of the little girl's nose and pinched it.

'That is your nose,' she says. 'Can you feel it?'

'Yes,' says the poor little girl.

'You must go along the road into the forest till you come to a fallen tree; then you must turn to your left, and then follow your nose and you will find her,' says the stepmother. 'Now, be off with you, lazy one. Here is some food for you to eat by the way.' She gave the little girl a bundle wrapped up in a towel.

The little girl wanted to go into the shed to tell the mouseykin she was going to Baba Yaga, and to ask what she should do. But she looked back, and there was the stepmother at the door watching her. So she had to go straight on.

She walked along the road through the forest till she came to the fallen tree. Then she turned to the left. Her nose was still hurting where the stepmother had pinched it, so she knew she had to go straight ahead. She was just setting out when she heard a little noise under the fallen tree.

'Scratch – scratch.'

And out jumped the little mouse, and sat up in the road in front of her.

'O mouseykin, mouseykin,' says the little girl,

'my stepmother has sent me to her sister. And that is Baba Yaga, the bony-legged, the witch, and I do not know what to do.'

'It will not be difficult,' says the little mouse, 'because of your kind heart. Take all the things you find in the road, and do with them what you like. Then you will escape from Baba Yaga, and everything will be well.'

'Are you hungry, mouseykin?' said the little girl.

'I could nibble, I think,' says the little mouse.

The little girl unfastened the towel, and there was nothing in it but stones. That was what the stepmother had given the little girl to eat by the way.

'Oh, I'm so sorry,' says the little girl. 'There's nothing for you to eat.'

'Isn't there?' said mouseykin, and as she looked at them the little girl saw the stones turn to bread and jam. The little girl sat down on the fallen tree, and the little mouse sat beside her, and they ate bread and jam until they were not hungry any more.

'Keep the towel,' says the little mouse; 'I think it will be useful. And remember what I said about the things you find on the way. And now goodbye,' says he.

'Goodbye,' says the little girl, and runs along.

As she was running along she found a nice new handkerchief lying in the road. She picked it up and took it with her. Then she found a little bottle of oil. She picked it up and took it with her. Then she found some scraps of meat.

'Perhaps I'd better take them too,' she said; and she took them.

Then she found a gay blue ribbon, and she took that. Then she found a little loaf of good bread, and she took that too.

'I daresay somebody will like it,' she said.

And then she came to the hut of Baba Yaga, the bony-legged, the witch. There was a high fence round it with big gates. When she pushed them open they squeaked miserably, as if it hurt them to move. The little girl was sorry for them.

'How lucky,' she says, 'that I picked up the bottle of oil!' and she poured the oil into the hinges of the gate.

Inside the railing was Baba Yaga's hut, and it stood on hen's legs and walked about the yard. And in the yard there was standing Baba Yaga's servant, and she was crying bitterly because of the tasks Baba Yaga set her to do. She was crying bitterly and wiping her eyes on her petticoat.

'How lucky,' says the little girl, 'that I picked up a handkerchief!' And she gave the handkerchief to Baba Yaga's servant, who wiped her eyes on it and smiled through her tears.

Close by the hut was a huge dog, very thin, gnawing a dry crust.

'How lucky,' says the little girl, 'that I picked

up a loaf!' And she gave the loaf to the dog, and he gobbled it up and licked his lips.

The little girl went bravely up to the hut and knocked on the door.

'Come in,' says Baba Yaga.

The little girl went in, and there was Baba Yaga, the bony-legged, the witch, sitting weaving at a loom. In a corner of the hut was a thin black cat watching a mouse-hole.

'Good-day to you, auntie,' says the little girl, trying not to tremble.

'Good-day to you, niece,' says Baba Yaga.

160

'My stepmother has sent me to you to ask for a needle and thread to mend a shirt.'

'Very well,' says Baba Yaga, smiling, and showing her iron teeth. 'You sit down here at the loom, and go on with my weaving, while I go and get you the needle and thread.'

The little girl sat down at the loom and began to weave.

Baba Yaga went out and called to her servant, 'Go, make the bath hot and scrub my niece. Scrub her clean. I'll make a dainty meal of her.'

The servant came in for the jug. The little girl begged her, 'Be not too quick in making the fire, and carry the water in a sieve.' The servant smiled, but said nothing, because she was afraid of Baba Yaga. But she took a very long time about getting the bath ready.

Baba Yaga came to the window and asked, 'Are you weaving, little niece? Are you weaving, my pretty?'

'I am weaving, auntie,' says the little girl.

When Baba Yaga went away from the window, the little girl spoke to the thin black cat who was watching the mouse-hole.

'What are you doing, thin black cat?'

'Watching for a mouse,' says the thin black cat. 'I haven't had any dinner for three days.'

'How lucky,' says the little girl, 'that I picked

up the scraps of meat!' And she gave them to the thin black cat. The thin black cat gobbled them up, and said to the little girl, 'Little girl, do you want to get out of this?'

'Catkin dear,' says the little girl, 'I do want to get out of this, for Baba Yaga is going to eat me with her iron teeth.'

'Well,' says the cat, 'I will help you.'

Just then Baba Yaga came to the window.

'Are you weaving, little niece?' she asked. 'Are you weaving, my pretty?'

'I am weaving, auntie,' says the little girl, working away, while the loom went clickety clack, clickety clack.

Baba Yaga went away.

Says the thin black cat to the little girl: 'You have a comb in your hair, and you have a towel. Take them and run for it while Baba Yaga is in the bath-house. When Baba Yaga chases after you, you must listen; and when she is close to you, throw away the towel, and it will turn into a big, wide river. It will take her a little time to get over that. But when she does, you must listen; and as soon as she is close to you throw away the comb, and it will sprout up into such a forest that she will never get through it at all.'

'But she'll hear the loom stop,' says the little girl.

'I'll see to that,' says the thin black cat.

The cat took the little girl's place at the loom.

Clickety clack, clickety clack; the loom never stopped for a moment.

The little girl looked to see that Baba Yaga was in the bath-house, and then she jumped down from the little hut on hen's legs, and ran to the gates as fast as her legs could flicker.

The big dog leapt up to tear her to pieces. Just as he was going to spring on her he saw who she was.

'Why, this is the little girl who gave me the loaf,' says he. 'A good journey to you, little girl'; and he lay down again with his head between his paws.

When she came to the gates they opened quietly, quietly, without making any noise at all, because of the oil she had poured into their hinges.

Outside the gates there was a little birch tree that beat her in the eyes so that she could not go by.

'How lucky,' says the little girl, 'that I picked up the ribbon!' And she tied up the birch tree with the pretty blue ribbon. And the birch tree was so pleased with the ribbon that it stood still, admiring itself, and let the little girl go by.

How she did run!

Meanwhile the thin black cat sat at the loom. Clickety clack, clickety clack, sang the loom; but you never saw such a tangle as the tangle made by the thin black cat.

And presently Baba Yaga came to the window.

'Are you weaving, little niece?' she asked. 'Are you weaving, my pretty?'

'I am weaving, auntie,' says the thin black cat, tangling and tangling, while the loom went clickety clack, clickety clack.

'That's not the voice of my little dinner,' says Baba Yaga, and she jumped into the hut, gnashing her iron teeth; and there was no little girl, but only the thin black cat, sitting at the loom, tangling and tangling the threads.

'Grr,' says Baba Yaga, and jumps for the cat, and begins banging it about. 'Why didn't you tear the little girl's eyes out?'

'In all the years I have served you,' says the cat, 'you have only given me one little bone; but the kind little girl gave me scraps of meat.'

Baba Yaga threw the cat into a corner, and went out into the yard.

'Why didn't you squeak when she opened you?' she asked the gates.

'Why didn't you tear her to pieces?' she asked the dog.

'Why didn't you beat her in the face, and not let her go by?' she asked the birch tree.

'Why were you so long in getting the bath ready? If you had been quicker, she never would have got away,' said Baba Yaga to the servant.

And she rushed about the yard, beating them all, and scolding at the top of her voice.

'Ah!' said the gates, 'in all the years we have served you, you never even eased us with water; but the kind little girl poured good oil into our hinges.'

'Ah!' said the dog, 'in all the years I've served you, you never threw me anything but burnt crusts; but the kind little girl gave me a good loaf.'

'Ah!' said the little birch tree, 'in all the years I've served you, you never tied me up, even with thread; but the kind little girl tied me up with a gay blue ribbon.'

'Ah!' said the servant, 'in all the years I've served you, you have never given me even a rag; but the kind little girl gave me a pretty handkerchief.'

Baba Yaga gnashed at them with her iron teeth. Then she jumped into the mortar and sat down. She drove it along with the pestle, and swept up her tracks with a besom, and flew off in pursuit of the little girl.

The little girl ran and ran. She put her ear to the ground and listened. Bang, bang, bangety bang! she could hear Baba Yaga beating the mortar with the pestle. Baba Yaga was quite close. There she was, beating with the pestle and sweeping with the besom, coming along the road.

As quickly as she could, the little girl took

out the towel and threw it on the ground. And the towel grew bigger and bigger, and wetter and wetter, and there was a deep, broad river between Baba Yaga and the little girl.

The little girl turned and ran on. How she ran!

Baba Yaga came flying up in the mortar. But the mortar could not float in the river with Baba Yaga inside. She drove it in, but only got wet for her trouble. Tongs and pokers tumbling down a chimney are nothing to the noise she made as she gnashed her iron teeth. She turned home, and went flying back to the little hut on hen's legs. Then she got together all her cattle and drove them to the river.

'Drink, drink!' she screamed at them; and the cattle drank up all the river to the last drop. And Baba Yaga, sitting in the mortar, drove it with the pestle, and swept up her tracks with the besom, and flew over the dry bed of the river and on in pursuit of the little girl.

The little girl put her ear to the ground and listened. Bang, bang, bangety bang! She could hear Baba Yaga beating the mortar with the pestle. Nearer and nearer came the noise, and there was Baba Yaga, beating with the pestle and sweeping with the besom, coming along the road close behind.

The little girl threw down the comb, and it

grew bigger and bigger, and its teeth sprouted up into a thick forest, thicker than this forest where we live – so thick that not even Baba Yaga could force her way through. And Baba Yaga, gnashing her teeth and screaming with rage and disappointment, turned round and drove away home to her little hut on hen's legs.

The little girl ran on home. She was afraid to go in and see her stepmother, so she ran into the shed.

Scratch, scratch! Out came the little mouse.

'So you got away all right, my dear,' says the little mouse. 'Now run in. Don't be afraid. Your father is back, and you must tell him all about it.'

The little girl went into the house.

'Where have you been?' says her father; 'and why are you so out of breath?'

The stepmother turned yellow when she saw her, and her eyes glowed, and her teeth ground together until they broke.

But the little girl was not afraid, and she went to her father and climbed on his knee, and told him everything just as it had happened. And when the old man knew that the stepmother had sent his little daughter to be eaten by Baba Yaga, he was so angry that he drove her out of the hut, and ever afterwards lived alone with the little girl. Much better it was for both of them.

'And the little mouse?' said Ivan.

'The little mouse,' said old Peter, 'came and lived in the hut, and every day it used to sit up on the table and eat crumbs, and warm its paws on the little girl's glass of tea.'

This story by Arthur Ransome is a retelling of the Russian fairy tale.

Sweets from a Stranger

First, the girl.

Tina Halliday, age eleven, almost black hair, waving at the ends. Brown eyes, tall for her age, quite pretty (but a nail-biter), good enough at most school subjects, very good at badminton (three trophies – and, if she won tonight, possibly a fourth soon to come).

Next, the car. Black Jaguar saloon, recent model, fawn leather upholstery, paintwork shining in the drizzly evening light.

And last, the driver of the car —

No, but wait. We will meet him a little later.

The black Jaguar was being driven slowly and badly. It lurched along the suburban street seeming to catch its breath, sneeze, then accelerate to all of fifteen miles an hour – then slow again. It came to a corner and took it in bites and nibbles, uncertainly, inexpertly.

169

Tina saw the car. She thought, That driver could be drunk. She moved closer to a low brick wall with a hedge. If the worst came to the worst – if the driver lost control – she could easily hop over the wall and be safe.

The car slowed. Now it seemed to be aiming at her: following her. Tina gripped her badminton racket tightly. She felt the first flutter of fear. The street was deserted. She thought, That car is coming for *me*.

The car almost stopped, right beside her, grating one wheel rim against the curb. Panic jumped into Tina's throat. When the car's window slid down, she thought, Shall I run? But her knees and legs felt weak.

A high-pitched voice, a man's voice, came through the open window. 'Little girl! Little girl! Do you want a ride in my car?'

Very loudly and distinctly, Tina said, 'No! I do not!' She thought, I'll give him 'little girl' if he tries anything on. 'Badminton Builds Bionic Biceps,' she murmured, and tried to smile.

The voice said, 'But – but it's a nice car. Wouldn't you like a ride?'

Tina said – almost shouted, 'No! Go away!'

The panic was leaving her. A part of her mind was almost giggling. If only Mum could see this! A classic scene! The thing she had been warned against even when she was tiny! 'Bad Stranger Man trying

170

to get Nice Little Girl into Big Wicked Car!' Next thing, he'd be offering her a sweetie . . .

The Jaguar wheezed as the driver over-revved the engine. It lurched and bumbled along beside her. The man inside – she could not see his face – said, 'Little girl! Wouldn't you like a sweetie? I've got some sweeties!'

At this, Tina began laughing. She laughed so much that she bent over in the middle. 'You're too much!' she choked. 'Really you are! Sweeties! A nice ride, and you've got some *sweeties*, too!'

The man said something that stopped her laughing. '*Please*,' he said. '*Please!*'

There was complete despair in his voice.

'Don't go away!' he said. She could see a sort of agony in the way his body stretched towards her. 'Don't go away! I don't *understand* anything . . . I don't know what to *do* . . .'

Tina, knowing she was behaving foolishly, went closer to the car, bent down and looked through the window. Even now she could not see the man. The instrument lights showed her only that he was small. Nothing else.

'They told me girls and boys liked sweets,' the man said, hopelessly. 'Crystallized fruits . . .' His voice was high and husky. 'They told me all sorts of things, but nothing helps. If only *you* would help . . .'

Tina told herself: You must be mad! – and got into the car.

Now she could see the man's head. It was turned away from her, bowed. Small man, small head.

'I don't know,' the man said. He made a gesture, a defeated throwing-out of his arm and hand. Tina saw the hand.

It was like a claw. It had only three fingers. There was skin that was not skin. There was dark, glossy hairiness.

The panic came back – leapt into her throat – choked her, froze her, numbed her.

'Nothing's working, nothing's going right,' the man said, in his high, rustling, despairing voice. Tina could not speak. She could only look at the hand, the dreadful hand.

He must have seen the whites of her eyes or the terrified O of her mouth, for he snatched his hand away, produced a glove and clumsily put it on. The glove had five fingers. Tina thought, Two of them must be padded. Still she could not move or speak. She made a gasping sound.

'I'm an invader,' the man said, as if replying to her sound. 'An invader. Come to conquer you. But it's not working.'

Tina coughed and forced her voice to work. 'An invader?' she said.

'Invading Earth,' the man said, dully. 'Your planet.'

'Where do you come from?' Tina said.

'Out there.' He waved his gloved hand vaguely upwards. 'Not from a planet: our home planet was finished thousands of years ago. We made our own world. We're having trouble with it. Not enough fuel, not enough ores and minerals, not enough of anything. Your planet has the things we need, so we're invading . . . But I don't know, I don't know . . .'

I'm not dreaming, Tina thought, This is real. It is happening. Escape! Run away! But she did not want to go.

'Look,' the man said. 'All I want to do is to stop being an invader. To go home. They told me things – told me what to do, what to say – but nothing fits, nothing goes right.'

'I don't see how I can help,' Tina said. 'I mean, what can I do?'

'Take me to a telephone. Get me a number, a particular number, I have it here —'

'But there's a telephone box just down the road, you passed it —'

'I couldn't make it work. They told me to use it, they told me how to use it; I did everything right, but it wouldn't work.'

'Come with me,' Tina said. Now she was no longer frightened, just very curious. 'Get out of the car. No, you must switch off the engine – that's right. And don't leave the keys in. Stop shaking, there's nothing to be afraid of. No, get out *your* side, there's no need to climb over the seats. Now close the door. Try again. Give it a good slam. Good. Take my arm. Come on.'

They reached the telephone box. The man walked as if his legs made him uneasy. He shook and trembled. Tina had to hold him up. He was not as tall as she.

The telephone would not work. 'Out of order,' Tina said, with a shrug.

'What does that mean?' the man said.

'Only that it doesn't work.'

'They never told us about "Out of Order",' the man said, dully.

'Wait a second!' Tina saw there was a coin jammed in the little slot. She managed to force the jammed coin in. Now the telephone worked. She dialled the number the man gave her. A high-pitched voice answered. The man took the handset – he held it the wrong way round at first – and spoke.

'Mission completed,' he said. Then, 'What? Oh. Oh. Well, I *can't* complete it any more than I *have* completed it, I can't go on *any longer* . . . What? No, no, I don't care, it's no good telling me that. Completed or uncompleted, I'm going home.'

He put the receiver back on the hook, sighed,

and said, 'Well, I'm not the only one. Several others have failed too and *they're* going home.'

Now Tina could see his face, for the first time, by the light of a street lamp. It was a horrible face, a waxwork mask – a face no more human than one of those plastic, jointed dolls. Though the mouth had lips, it was really only a movable hole. The skin – but it was not skin – was too tight over the cheek-bones, too loose at the ears. And the ears were waxen, unreal. The hair began and ended too sharply. It did not grow from the scalp; it was fitted to it. A wig.

She shuddered. '*Why?*' she demanded. 'Why did they dress you up like this? I mean, if you're an invader, why couldn't you look like an invader? – someone frightening and threatening and, what's the word, indomitable? You're just a – a mess. I'm sorry, but you are.'

'They – my masters – wanted us to be friendly invaders,' the man explained. 'Not monsters: people like yourselves. People who use telephones and drive cars and wear clothes. But it went wrong, of course. Everything's gone wrong.'

'What are you really like?' Tina said.

The man shifted uneasily. 'Probably you'd think us hideous,' he said. 'You might hate us if you saw us as we really are.'

'But you don't think *me* hideous?' Tina said,

176

smiling. She knew she had a nice smile. Her smile faded as she saw the man's eyes (too big to fit the false eyelids) change, grow cautious and look away.

'Well . . .' he said. 'Well . . .'

'You *do* think me hideous?' Tina said, amazed.

'You're so different, that's what it is. So very different from us. Your eyes are so small and pale, and your skin is white, and your hair grows in the wrong places —'

'I see,' Tina said, pursing her lips.

'I hope I haven't given offence?'

'Not at all. Do go on,' she said, stiffly.

'Different,' the man said. 'Things are so different where I come from! Perhaps a bit better. A lot better in some ways.' He began to speak enthusiastically. 'We don't need to use telephones when we want to speak to each other: we just tune into minds. We don't need these complicated great machines, these cars, to travel in. We don't cover ourselves with layers of fabric to keep the weather out —'

'You go naked, I suppose?' Tina said, acidly.

'Well, we don't find it necessary to wrap ourselves in coloured rags! But perhaps you do it because you'd be so ugly if you didn't — Oh, I beg your pardon —'

'Don't mind *me*,' Tina said, coldly. 'A pity, though, that you can't seem to cope in your superior world! Pity you have to go round invading people! Or,' she added spitefully, '*attempting* to invade them!'

'Our world must survive,' the man said, quietly. 'It's a beautiful and wonderful world. It must be saved!'

Tina said, 'Hmm.'

'The most beautiful! The most wonderful!' the man insisted. 'If only you could see it for yourself! Then you'd understand!'

'I'm sure you're right,' Tina said, distantly. She looked at her watch. 'Lord! I'm late! I must go! The time!'

'On our world, we control time,' the man told her. 'We always have time . . .' A thought struck him. 'Come with me! See my world! Don't worry about time – stay as long as you like and I promise you'll be back here only a minute or so from now! Come with me!'

His dark eyes blazed at her from the mask of his face. The mask was stupid: the eyes were not.

For the second time Tina told herself: You must be mad! Out loud, she said, 'All right, then. Show me your world.'

She felt herself twisted, racked, stretched, flung apart – and thought, This is the journey, then.

'This is my face,' he said. The mock-human mask was gone. Huge, dark, liquid eyes looked at

178

her from the furred face – the face of a cat, but not
a cat, not a seal, not an otter, not any Earth animal.
She saw the neat, flowing body, covered in dense
fur, dark grey and tipped with silver. She saw the
high forehead, the mobile mouth (He's smiling!
she thought, So that's how they look when they
smile!). No tail. Useful three-fingered hands. A
mobile, businesslike thumb.

'There is my world,' he said. Through the
glassy bubble of nothingness that separated them
from the stars, a world gleamed and glittered in
the blackness, coming closer and closer impossibly
fast – a huge, complicated globe, jewelled with a
million tiny lights, sprinkled with clouds.

'Shana,' he said. 'That is Shana. I am a Shanad. In
the heart of the world, there is a city called Ro-yil.
Can you say those words?'

She found that she could. Her mouth spoke
them for her in a tongue her brain did not know.
She tried out this new gift. 'What is your name?'

'Talis,' he said.

'Rhymes with Palace,' Tina said, vaguely. There
was so much to look at, the glittering world was
rushing at them —

'There,' said Talis. 'We have landed. Get out.
I will show you the city first.'

He hurried her to the edge of a vast square shaft,
took her hand, and made her fall, endlessly, through
a tunnel of lights and textures, fleeting shapes and

sounds. She wanted to scream; but Talis's calm face was beside her, his hand held hers, his voice spoke to her.

They seemed to meet some sort of invisible cushion. The sensation was like that of being in a lift, slowing violently.

And then they were in the city of Ro-yil.

The city hung, a sphere within a sphere, from glistening filaments, pulsing with light. ('They are avenues,' Talis explained, matter-of-factly, 'rather like the one we are standing in.') Towers soared, glassy and magnificent. Plants taller than Earth trees sang softly. There were Shanads everywhere, many in glassy bubbles like that which had carried Tina and Talis from Earth. The bubbles seemed to move instantly from place to place. 'Hoverflies . . . fireflies,' Tina murmured.

'What?' Talis said.

'Beautiful,' she replied. 'Wonderful, beautiful, magnificent . . . !'

A crystal bubble drifted by. It was empty. 'Tsa!' said Talis; the bubble stopped by them. 'Ata-al!' he said and the side of the bubble split open. 'Get in,' he said. 'I'll take you to my home.'

Tina memorized the words and tried to understand how Talis drove the bubble. There was no time. The city hurtled for a split-second, then gently slowed. Tina gasped. Talis smiled. 'You like my city, then?' His voice had changed. Now it was confident, laughing, sure.

Tina could only reply, 'Marvellous!' Then, 'This bubble,' she said, 'it's the same as the one that brought us here, isn't it?'

'The same. It can take you anywhere! Anywhere in the universe! But who would want to leave *this*?' He swept his arm at the jewelled city, the crystalline towers of pearl and jet, aquamarine and turquoise, strung together with luminous silver threads . . .

'Home,' he said. 'Come.'

A door opened in a glassy golden wall.

She entered and saw humans.

The door closed and Talis was gone.

There were perhaps twenty of them. The room was not big enough. They stared at her, silently. Then a raggedly dressed woman with a tired face came to Tina and said, 'Oh dear. Poor you. And so young.'

'But Talis said – Talis promised —'

'Oh, I dare say he did. I dare say he told you he can control time and all that . . . And you fell for it. Felt sorry for him, didn't you? Felt you had to help? Those big dark eyes of theirs . . . And you fell for it. So did I, years ago. I was a District Nurse. Do you know Hove? And Brighton? That was where I was —'

A young man, his clothes falling to pieces,

snorted, 'Never mind about Hove and Brighton. We've had enough of them.' He turned his back on the District Nurse and said, 'What's your name, then? Tina? Tina. You're right in it now. Up to the neck. Like the rest of us. There's lots of us, you know. Not just this room: the whole building.' He shrugged despairingly. To the District Nurse he said, 'You explain to her.'

'You're a hostage, dear,' the woman said. 'At least, that's the way we work it out. I mean, they want to invade Earth, but they can't. You see, they want metals and minerals and I-don't-know-what from Earth; but their weapons won't work *without* the metals and minerals and I-don't-know-whats. So they're stuck, aren't they?'

'What do you mean, hostages?' Tina said. Another man joined the group and answered. 'They're going to use us instead of weapons,' he said. 'They'll tell Earth they've got us. If Earth won't give them the things they want, they'll threaten to kill us, you see? They'll *barter* us! When they've got enough of us.'

Tina said, 'But – but they can't! I've got to go home!'

The young man told Tina, 'Cheer up, you're not dead yet. No good crying.'

Tina swallowed her sobs and said, 'How long have you been here?'

'He's been here longest,' the nurse said, pointing

to a man huddled in a corner. 'Seven years. Old misery, he is. You won't get anything out of him. Given up speaking to anyone years ago.'

'Why don't you escape?' Tina said.

'Might be difficult, don't you think?' the young man said, cynically. 'I mean, we don't *look* much like them, do we? We'd be a bit *noticeable* outside, wouldn't we? Anyhow, if you think you can get out, have a go. Ah, food!'

A door in the wall opened: a gleaming box slid in. Immediately everyone – even the crouched man – came to life. They grabbed and gobbled, crammed their mouths, bargained noisily over swaps.

Tina thought, You're a shabby lot. She ate the food. It looked strange but tasted good. The things that looked like crystallized fruits were best of all. She saved some, hiding them in her pocket. She thought, They've given in; I won't. I'll learn everything I can, and hoard food and wait for the right moment: then I'll escape . . .

Nobody showed much interest when, three days later, Tina emptied the food box, climbed into it, and escaped the room.

Now she was at large in the city. The Shanad words she had learned from Talis were still in her mind. She had practised them and knew them well. But that was about all she knew.

Soon, she did not even know what she had hoped

to gain by escaping. The Shanads thronging the city of Ro-yil neither helped nor hindered her. No sirens screamed, no vehicles dashed, no hard-faced law-enforcers pounced. The Shanads (to Tina, they all looked the same) ignored her. Their large, dark, intelligent eyes looked at her – then, deliberately, looked away.

'A bubble . . .' she said to herself. 'That's what I must have.' A bubble drifted beside her. 'Tsa!' she said. 'Ata-al!' She sat in the bubble, trying to find a knob or a lever or anything at all that would make it go. She failed. Shanads passed by, not looking or caring. She began to cry. She got out of the bubble and walked blindly, endlessly, through the gorgeous city.

She reached the shafts by accident. One shaft had brought her down from the surface of the world to the city; now she saw a twin shaft. Shanads walked into its entrance and went up. Up to the surface! 'One step nearer home,' Tina said, entered the shaft, and flew to the surface.

She found herself looking at white clouds in a green sky. Beyond, she saw darkness and in the darkness, stars and planets. 'One of you is Earth,' she said. She looked for a bubble. This time, she would not give up. This time, she would go home.

She saw a bubble. It was stationary. In front of it, two furry little things, charming, fat and jolly, rolled on the ground. They were smaller than Shanads, much smaller —

'Ah!' said Tina. '*Children!*'

'Tsa!' she hissed; and got into the bubble. The child Shanads rolled and squeaked, pounced and wrestled, outside. 'Ata-al!' she said. The magic word once again failed to have any effect. She knocked on the wall of the bubble to attract the children's attention. They looked up at her. Their eyes were beautiful.

Tina said – her mind and voice struggling for the words, 'I'm a friend. I need your help. I'm a friend! Help me!'

The children stared. One made a gurgling noise that must have been giggling.

'Look,' Tina said, 'I've got this lovely bubble, but I can't seem to work it. Wouldn't you like to show me how to work it?'

Both children giggled. Neither moved.

'Look, suppose you get in with me, and show me what to do, then we can go for a ride!'

The Shanad children linked paws and stared at her, still giggling.

Tina remembered the crystallized fruits in her pocket. 'I'll give you these!' she cried. 'One for each of you! *Two* each!'

And suddenly the Shanad children were running away, running very fast. They ran until they reached an adult Shanad, then stopped and pointed at Tina. She could hear what they were saying.

'. . . wanted to take us for a *ride*!' one said.

'In a nice bubble!' said the other.

'Offered us *sweets*!' said the first. 'Us! As if we'd take sweets from strangers!'

They pointed their fingers and giggled, loudly and scornfully. They jumped up and down, delighted with themselves.

And then Talis was there, with many other Shanads.

They took Tina back to the room.

One day, perhaps, the Shanads will make contact with Earth. Until then, Tina will at least be fed. The things that look like crystallized fruits are delicious, at first.

Later, you grow tired of them.

This story is by Nicholas Fisk.

186

Lost Vanya

This may be true or it may not; but the person who told it me said it was true.

There were once two cousins named Vanya and Misha. They had been brought up together, and had always been closer than brothers. When people saw Vanya, then they looked round for Misha; when they met Misha, they called out a greeting to Vanya, knowing he couldn't be far away.

Vanya's and Misha's favourite game was boasting to each other of what they would do when they were grown men. In bed, before they fell asleep; in fields, lying idle; at the dinner-table, when they should have been eating, they would whisper together.

'I shall build my own house, and keep my own cattle, and be a big man in the village,' Misha said.

'Your house won't be as big as mine,' Vanya

would answer, 'and you won't have as many cattle. And I shall breed horses too.'

Then they would giggle and punch each other, and try to think of other ways to outdo each other.

'I shall travel far away – to Africa, to England, to Spain!' said Misha. 'I shall come back with things no-one has ever seen! And everyone will want to buy them, and I shall be rich and build a palace!'

'I shall go further and bring back more and be richer and build two palaces!' said Vanya.

They grew to be young men, but they were still friends and they still played the boasting-game. 'I shall marry the most beautiful girl in the world,' said Misha. 'Other men will faint to see her. I shall marry her, and we shall have fifty children and be the happiest family on earth!'

'I shall marry a girl twice as beautiful, and have a hundred and fifty children!' said Vanya. 'I'm bound to be happy, because in that crowd I shall never be lonely.'

But before Misha was nineteen, he died, of consumption. As Misha lay in his coffin, Vanya tucked a full bottle of vodka in beside him, to help his friend keep away the cold of the earth. They buried Misha beneath a birch-tree in the graveyard, and it was a long, long time before people stopped expecting to see him at Vanya's side. It was even longer before Vanya stopped looking for him there.

But all things pass; and Vanya went on growing

older. In his twenty-second year, he asked Elenia to marry him, and she said yes. No-one fainted at the sight of her, but she was very pretty, and Vanya was as happy as he could have been if his old boast had come true.

On the day of the wedding, they set off in carts decorated with flowers, and everyone was happy until they passed the graveyard. There Vanya saw the birch-tree beneath which Misha lay buried. He remembered their game, and realized that here he was, on his wedding day, making his boast good, in part, at least; while poor Misha had been cold and buried for years, with no hope of matching him. He had far surpassed Misha, just as he had always sworn he would do, but had never believed that he could. Vanya felt that he should apologize to Misha because he was alive and Misha was dead. So he stopped the cart, climbed down, and walked alone into the graveyard.

His bride, and their two families, and all the guests, watched him from the road, and called to him to hurry. He waved and said that he only wanted a minute, just a minute . . .

Looking down at the grave, feeling foolish, feeling tears behind his eyes, he muttered, 'Misha . . . can you hear me? Here I am – Vanya – you remember – and it's my wedding day! So I've come to tell you that, Misha . . . and to wish you well . . . wherever you are . . .'

The ground at his feet gave a quiver, and the grave opened. There lay Misha, in his coffin, looking just as he had when they'd buried him, except that he was whiter. And more gaunt. He raised an arm towards Vanya, and in his hand there was a bottle of vodka.

'Vanya, my friend, bless you! You remember me, though I've been dead so long, even on your wedding day you remember me! You would make me cry, Vanushka, if I could cry. And here is the vodka you gave me – I owe you so much! Please, Vanya, little brother, come and drink a glass of vodka with me on your wedding day.'

'But, Misha – you're dead!'

'Does that matter? Do you fear me now, because I'm dead? Oh, Vanushka; did I ever give you any reason to fear me?' And Misha held out his blue-white, bone hand for Vanya to take. 'Don't deny me this moment of friendship,' the dead man pleaded. 'I always believed I would drink a toast to you on your wedding day. Stay a few moments, Vanushka; long enough to drink a glass and speak a word or two.'

How could Vanya refuse? 'Just a minute, then,' he said, and took Misha's hand.

The grip of the dead hand was hard and cold. With a strong pull, Misha drew Vanya forward into the grave, as if he drew him over the threshold of a house – while Misha himself retreated further

in. The wedding-guests, watching from the road, raised a cry of distress as they saw Vanya step into the earth.

All light vanished from Vanya's sight as the grave closed; but then a blue light, like the blue flames of corpse-candles, lit Misha's death-head.

Vanya said, 'When I put that bottle in your coffin, I never expected to share it!' They were crammed together in the narrow space – the grave is a small house. The cold moisture of the earth soaked through Vanya's clothes, and violet worms wriggled from the walls in the blue light.

'To you and your wife on your wedding day!' said Misha. 'May you have a long and happy life together, and a houseful of children!' He drank from the bottle, and passed it to Vanya.

Vanya would have liked to wipe the neck of the bottle, but he didn't want to hurt his friend's feelings. 'To me,' he said, and bravely drank before passing the bottle back.

'Who is your wife? Did I know her?' Misha asked. The walls of damp earth soaked up his voice, and the sound was like mice whispering in a nest.

'Yes; she is Elenia Gregorovna. And now, Misha, I must —'

'Ah! A beautiful girl – even when I knew her, you could see she would be a beauty! Congratulations, Vanushka! A toast to Elenia Gregorovna! Long life

and good health to her, a child every year to her!'
And he drank, and handed the bottle to Vanya.

'I'll gladly drink to that,' Vanya said, 'but then
I must go, Misha. They are waiting for me, you
know, and I said I would only stay —'

'Drink, drink!' said Misha.

'I will, but . . . You will open the door and
let me out, won't you, Misha?'

'Vanya! Do you think I will keep you here?
I – your friend?'

'No, of course you wouldn't!' Vanya said, and
laughed, and drank to his bride. 'Here's your bottle,
Misha – good of you to keep it until I came! Now
do your trick and open the door —'

'One more drink,' Misha said.

'Oh no, Misha . . . You must understand how
nervous I am, sitting here in a grave; you understand, Misha. It's not the same as in the old days.
And my bride will think I've deserted her. I'd love
to stay and chat, but really I can't —'

'Just one drink to me,' said the dead man. 'Won't
you, on your wedding day, spare just a moment to
drink a toast to me?'

Vanya took the bottle and said, 'Here's to my
friend, Misha, my friend still, though he's dead.
May he lie at peace in his grave . . . Is that good?'

'Very good,' Misha said. 'Thank you, Vanushka.
You make me happy.' And he watched with pleasure as Vanya drank to him and, taking the bottle

back, he drank too. 'Now, I suppose you must go,' he said sadly. 'Goodbye, Vanya. I shall never see you again.'

Vanya felt tears come to his eyes. 'In Heaven, surely?'

'No,' said Misha, still more sadly. He leaned forward and hugged Vanya, smelling strongly of earth. He kissed Vanya's cheeks with cold lips. 'Goodbye, goodbye,' he said, so sadly that Vanya almost cried.

Daylight lit the grave, and Vanya knew that the grave had opened. Sad for his friend, but still relieved to be escaping into the clear air, he clambered from the grave, calling goodbye. Before he could blink, the grave had closed again, and was as it had been before; as if it had never opened.

Vanya straightened and stretched and turned to the road where his wedding party was waiting – and the road was quite empty; no people, no carts, no horses.

He must have been longer than he'd thought, and they'd gone on without him. He ran from the graveyard to the church – but the church was deserted too. No-one was near it.

'They think I've run away,' he thought, in a panic. 'Elenia will be angry with me.' And he ran from the church to the village. At least the running warmed him. He was so cold after being in the grave that he couldn't feel the sun.

'Has the wedding party come this way?' he shouted to a man in a field.

'What wedding party?' the man asked. 'Who are you?'

'Who are you?' Vanya asked, for the man was a stranger. They stood staring at each other.

'Who marries at this time of year?' said the man.

'It's summer!' Vanya exclaimed. The end of summer, when the harvest was in – the best time of all for marrying and feasting!

'Summer!' said the man, and sounded so surprised that Vanya looked around and saw – how could he not have noticed? – that it was not summer. The fields were bare and hard; the sky over them was grey. Only the pine trees had leaves. The chill of the grave had followed him out of the earth.

'Misha, what have you done to me?'

He walked along the hard road to his village – but it was not his village any more. There was not a face that he knew. Houses that had been new that morning were now old, and there were houses that he had never seen. He knocked at doors, and the people looked at him as if he was a stranger. He asked for Elenia Gregorovna, and was taken to her, but it was a middle-aged woman, not his Elenia.

'Misha, Misha, why did you do this?' he said. The people asked him what he meant, and when he tried to explain, they became afraid and drew away from him.

'It's him, it's Lost Vanya!' said the middle-aged Elenia. 'My great-grandmother,' she said, leaning towards Vanya, 'was named Elenia Gregorovna and when she was a young girl she went to be married to a man named Vanya. But at the churchyard he got down to visit the grave of a dead friend . . . he vanished in front of their eyes, and never came back. Are you him? Are you Lost Vanya?'

But Vanya turned away from her, saying, 'Misha, why have you done this to me?' The people followed him, and saw him leave the village and walk the road to the churchyard. Poor wanderer; homeless, graveless.

He went into the churchyard and to an old birch-tree. Under it was a forgotten grave, so old that no-one remembered who was buried there, or cared for it. 'Misha —?' said Lost Vanya, and then, as his foot touched the grave, he crumbled away, and was truly lost.

This story is by Susan Price.

196

William's Double Life

It happened that William, unusually enough, was
thrown upon his own resources. It was the holi-
days and all the other Outlaws were away from
home. Douglas had gone to stay with an aunt at
the seaside. He had been bored at the prospect and
the visit was not turning out any more enjoyable
than he had thought it would. His only consolation
was that his aunt was finding it even more trying
than he. Ginger had gone with his family to stay at
a boarding house. Already the oldest resident of the
boarding house had taken such a dislike to Ginger's
rendering of 'Let's Go Round to Alice's House', that
he had issued an ultimatum to the effect that either
Ginger or he must depart at once and for ever. He
had left it to the boarding house proprietress to
choose between them and she had done so. She
had chosen the oldest resident. Ginger's parents
were already packing . . .

Henry was taking part in a camping holiday with some cousins of the same age and disposition as himself. The young schoolmaster who had organized the expedition had meant to camp in the same place for the whole fortnight, but as events turned out, they had moved on after each night. They had not moved on of their own accord. They had left a train of infuriated farmers behind them in their passage across England. The young schoolmaster had returned home with a nervous breakdown and had already had two successors.

And so William was thrown upon his own resources.

Though much relieved that his own family was not taking a holiday (for William hated to be torn from his familiar pursuits and the familiar fields and ditches of his native village) he was for the first two days rather at a loss as to what to do without the other Outlaws. And then he had an inspiration. An aquarium. He'd make an aquarium. He'd already made a zoo and a circus, he'd already organized greyhound racing (all without any striking success), but he'd never yet made an aquarium. He'd make an aquarium with two hundred inhabitants in a large pail (William's mind, like the minds of all great organizers, leapt ahead, arranging even the smallest detail). He'd start at once . . .

The first thing to do, of course, was to find a pail. He was prepared to go to any lengths to obtain one and had just conceived the bold design of carrying off the washing pail from under the cook's vigilant and hostile eyes, when to his amazement she offered it to him.

'That pail's just beginning to leak, Master William,' she said carelessly, 'if you'd like it for any of your contraptions you can have it.'

William accepted it coldly. It was disappointing to have screwed up his courage for a daring *coup* and then to find that the *coup* was unnecessary. Moreover, William preferred the cook as an enemy than a friend. Life was very dull to William when he and the cook were being polite to each other. However, he found a little comfort in making a bold daylight raid upon a workman's hod when actually in action in the workman's hand in order to obtain some mortar to mend the leak in the pail. The workman, welcoming the little diversion almost as much as did William, threw down the hod and pursued him unavailingly to the end of the road, showering threats and abuse in his wake, then returned, cheered and invigorated, to his work.

The pail was mended, filled with water and put into the shed to await its two hundred inhabitants.

And here William's troubles began. For the fish denizens of the neighbourhood were coy. They refused to enter the net that William held in the stream with such patience and jerked up at intervals with such sudden cunning. They ignored his worms obtained with great labour and at the expense of some of the choicest garden plants. They scorned his bent pins. In the course of two mornings' hard work, he caught only an old tin, a curtain hook and a bottle in his net and on his bent pin a bootlace and the remnants of a grimy shirt discarded by some passing tramp. William was not the boy lightly to abandon any idea he had once taken up, but it was just as despair was descending upon him that he remembered the pond in the garden of The Laburnums. The Laburnums was a largish house at the further end of the village and in its garden just beyond the orchard was a pond – a pond teeming with potential inhabitants of William's aquarium. William and the other Outlaws had discovered it about a year ago, but the owner had then been an irate colonel who had caught the Outlaws fishing in his pond and robbing his orchard and had inflicted such condign punishment that even those bold spirits had not wooed that particular adventure again. But it occurred now to William that he had seen a 'To Let' notice at the gate of The Laburnums and he set off at once – net, glass jar with string handle, worm, bent pin, stick and all – to reconnoitre. His impression turned out to be correct. There was a 'To Let' notice at the gate of The Laburnums. He did not enter boldly at the front gate because in his acquaintance of empty houses (and it was a wide one) there was generally a caretaker in possession, and caretakers, though content generally to doze their lives away in the kitchen, were, nevertheless, of a savage disposition when roused, and, like the wild buffaloes of Africa, attacked on sight.

So he walked down the road till he found the place in the hedge where a year ago a serviceable hole had been made by the frequent passage of the Outlaws' solid bodies. Time had healed the breach to a certain extent, but there was still room just to admit William with his accoutrements. Having scraped through the hole with only a few casualties (the loss of his worm, a hole in his net and a forest of scratches on his hands) William cautiously made his way to the orchard. It took him longer than it need have done to cross the orchard. The amount of apples William could consume during a leisurely stroll across an average-sized orchard would have astounded anyone of normal digestive capacities. At length, however, gorged and happy, he made his way to the pond. And the pond exceeded his wildest expectations. It teemed with inhabitants and inhabitants of an engagingly friendly and trusting disposition. They jostled each other for entrance to his net and those who fell through the hole seemed to struggle to get back again. They impaled themselves willingly upon his bent pin. They even placed themselves confidently in his bare hand. He fished there for over an hour. At last, carefully carrying his glass jar by its string handle and glowing with the pride of the successful hunter, he sauntered slowly back through the orchard. The apples delayed him again for some time, and when even William had reached his limit (a limit to be spoken of with bated breath) he stuffed his pockets and wandered homeward, mentally composing (slightly exaggerated) accounts of the affair to tell the other Outlaws on their return.

Then followed a blissful week for William. He went to The Laburnums with his jar every morning. He first spent an hour or so in the orchard. After that he staggered to the pond in a state of happy repletion, filled his jar from the teeming population of the pond, then, with appetite restored, returned to the orchard.

He felt that it was too good to last, and it was. At the end of a week he saw a large removing van entering the front gate. He made the most of that day. He ate so many apples that he went home in a state closely bordering on intoxication.

The next day, more from force of habit than anything else, he went to the house as usual with his jar, his fishing-rod, and what a week's hard wear had left of his net. He went without any definite plans. It was no longer that most exciting of playgrounds – an 'empty house'. It was now inhabited, owned and presumably guarded. He would be liable now at any minute to a descent from a ferocious inhabitant. He watched the house from the front gate for some time. Maids were cleaning windows, shaking out dusters, putting up curtains. An elderly woman with pince-nez and very elaborately-dressed hair was evidently the mistress of the house and she seemed to be in sole possession. That relieved William, who generally found women easier to deal with than men. The bustle within the house, too, reassured him. While they were cleaning windows and shaking out dusters and putting up curtains, they could not be making descents upon the pond and orchard. He might surely take this last day in his paradise.

He found it even more enjoyable than any of the others. He had decided that it must be his last day there, and yet the next morning he set off as usual with his jar and rod and net. He did this partly because the risk now attached to the proceeding enhanced it in his eyes, and partly because he'd only got one hundred of his two hundred fishes. He felt that a hundred fishes in that pond still belonged to him and in fetching them he was only claiming his rightful property.

It was a beautiful morning. The sun shone brightly on the pond and orchard. The apples seemed riper and more delicious than ever before, the inhabitants of the pond more guileless and trusting. After his customary fruitful journey through the orchard he sat as usual happily fishing by the side of the pond.

Then – it happened. It happened without the slightest warning. He heard no sound of her approach. Suddenly a hand was laid on his shoulder from behind and looking up with a start his eyes met the eyes of the woman with the pince-nez and elaborately-dressed hair. All about him were the signs of his guilt. His jar containing his morning's 'bag' stood on one side of him together with a little pile of apples gathered for refreshment in the intervals of fishing. On the other side of him lay a little heap of cores representing refreshment already taken. His pockets bulged with apples. His mouth was full of apple. He held a half-eaten apple in one hand and his rod in the other.

'You *naughty* little ruffian,' exploded his captor. 'How *dare* you trespass in my grounds and steal my fruit?'

William swallowed half an apple unmasticated and by means of a gentle wriggle experimented with the grip on his shoulder. He was an expert in grips. The gentlest of wriggles could tell him whether a grip was the sort of grip he could escape from or whether it wasn't. This one wasn't. It was, William generously allowed in his mind, an unusually good grip for a woman. So he abandoned himself to his fate, and contented himself with glaring at his captor with unblinking ferocity. He certainly wasn't a prepossessing sight. His face was streaked with mud. His collar (sodden and muddy) was awry. He had used his tie to repair his fishing rod. His legs were caked with mud up to the knees. His suit was so thickly covered with mud that its pattern was almost indiscernible. His captor's closer inspection evidently did nothing to modify the unfavourable opinion she had formed of him.

'What's your name?' she said sharply.

'William Brown,' said William.

He knew by experience that people always found out his name sooner or later and that to refuse to give it made ultimate proceedings more unpleasant.

'Very well,' said his captor meaningly, 'I shall call to see your father about it. Go away out of my garden at *once*.'

With great dignity William gathered up his jar of fishes, his net, stuffed the pile of apples into his pockets (his pockets held a good number of apples as William had made a convenient hole through which they could descend to the lining), kicked his pile of cores into the pond, put on his bedraggled cap, raised it as politely as he could considering his many burdens, stooped down to pick up a fish that the effort of raising his cap had displaced from his jar, and with a courteous 'Good mornin' ' walked very slowly and with an indescribable swagger across the orchard to the lawn, across the lawn to the front drive, and down to the front gate. He wasn't going to give away his hole to her. At the front gate he turned, raised his cap to her again, dropped his net and another fish, picked them up without any undue haste and strolled out into the road.

As he walked homewards he couldn't help thinking that he'd carried off the situation with something of an air. But that feeling of gratification was of short duration. She had said that she was going to tell his father, and he was pretty sure that a woman who could grip like that would be as good as her word. It meant, besides any other incidental unpleasantness, that an end would be put to his fishing activities and that, as likely as not, his aquarium would be thrown away. He still retained bitter memories of the wholesale destruction of a laboriously-acquired collection of insects that he had kept secretly in the spare room wardrobe until it was found and destroyed.

In a vague desire to propitiate authority he made an elaborate toilet for lunch – changing his socks and shoes, completely removing several layers of mud from his knees, brushing his suit, washing his face and hands, and severely punishing his hair. His mother greeted his appearance with a cry of horror: 'William, what a *sight* you are! What have you been doing?'

He murmured 'Fishin' ' rather distantly and sat down to his soup.

'Why didn't you wash and tidy your hair before

you came in to lunch?' continued his mother sternly.

'I did,' said William simply, and not only received apparently unmoved his elder brother's snort of derision, but also pretended not to notice his further challenge of the gesture of a cat perfunctorily washing its face with its paw. This was no moment for reprisals. Robert could wait. At any minute the woman with the hair and the pince-nez might come to report his morning's activities, and the less he embroiled himself with Authority in the meantime the better.

'You won't forget where you're going out to tea this afternoon, William, will you?' said his mother.

'No,' said William, sinking into yet deeper gloom.

He was going out to tea with the vicar. Occasionally the vicar, who disliked children intensely, but suffered from an over-active conscience, invited his more youthful parishioners to tea. He was a precise and tidy man and liked peace and quiet, and he hardly slept at all the night before such a party took place, but he felt that was part of his priestly duty and went through with it in the spirit of the early Christian martyrs. His youthful guests generally enjoyed their visits, partly because his wife made a peculiarly delicious brand of treacle cake, and partly because the vicar was entirely at a loss how to deal with the very young, and, given the right blending of guests, the affair could be trusted to develop into a very enjoyable riot. The only drawback of it in William's eyes was the long and painful process of cleansing and tidying to which he was subjected before he was declared fit to present himself at the Vicarage. On this occasion, despite William's own heroic efforts before lunch, the process lasted an hour, and it was after three when – clean and shining in his best suit, a gleaming Eton collar, a perfectly tied tie, neatly gartered stockings and radiant boots with tags tucked down inside – he was allowed to set off down the road towards the vicarage. He walked slowly. As all the other Outlaws were away from home, it wasn't likely to be a very exciting affair, but at any rate there would be the treacle cake – and the vicar. The vicar could always be counted upon for entertainment.

He was vaguely aware of a figure approaching him from the opposite direction, but beyond noting almost subconsciously that it was adult and feminine, he took no interest in it. He was surprised to find that it stopped in front of him. He looked up with a start. It was the woman with the pince-nez and the hair.

'Well,' she said grimly, 'I'm on my way to see your father.' Then she stopped and faltered. 'You – you *are* William Brown, aren't you?' she said uncertainly. William saw at once what had happened. He was so clean and tidy as to be almost unrecognizable as the hero of the morning's escapade. As she scanned his features still more closely he saw her uncertainty changing again to certainty. William's features were, after all, unmistakable.

'You *are*, aren't you?' she said.

And then William had an inspiration – or rather an *INSPIRATION* – or rather an INSPIRATION – the sort of INSPIRATION that comes to most of us only once in a lifetime, but that visited William more frequently.

Fixing her with a virtuous and mournful gaze, he said: 'No, I'm not William Brown. I'm his twin brother.'

Her severity vanished.

'I see,' she said. 'I could see a *strong* resemblance, but yet I was sure that there was some difference, though I couldn't have said what it was. He was very dirty and untidy, of course.'

'Yes,' agreed William sadly, 'I expect he was.'

'You're very alike in features though, aren't you?' she went on with interest. 'It must be difficult for people to tell you apart.'

'Yes,' agreed William, warming to his theme, 'lots of people can't tell us apart. His nose is just a bit longer. That's one way of telling us.'

'Yes,' she agreed still with great interest, 'I believe it is, now you mention it. And his ears stick out more.'

'Do they?' said William coldly.

'I'm just on my way to call on your parents to complain of your brother,' went on the lady, her interest turning to severity. 'I found him this morning trespassing in my garden, stealing my apples and catching fishes in my pond. Do you know about it?'

William wondered for a minute whether to know about it, and finally decided that it would be more effective to know about it than not to. His mournful and virtuous expression deepened.

'Yes,' he said, 'he told me about it. I was jus' comin' to – to see you about it.'

'Why?' said the lady.

'I was comin' to ask you to let him off jus' for this once,' said William more mournfully, more virtuously, than ever. 'I was goin' to ask you not to go an' see my father an' mother about him this time.'

It was quite evident that the lady was touched by his appeal.

'You don't want your dear parents troubled by it, I suppose?' she said.

'Yes,' said William, 'that's it. I don't want my dear parents troubled by it.'

She pondered deeply.

'I see,' she said. 'Well, your consideration for your parents does you credit – er – what is your name?'

211

'Algernon,' said William without a second's hesitation.

The name came in fact almost of its own accord. The vicar at his last tea party had tried to instil some order into a party that was rapidly degenerating into pandemonium by reading aloud a moral story from which as a child he had derived much profit and enjoyment. Though not received quite in the spirit he would have wished, it had certainly succeeded in riveting his guests' attention. The hero – a child with a singularly beautiful disposition – had been called Algernon. For weeks afterwards 'Algernon' had been the favourite epithet of abuse among the youngest set of the village.

'Algernon,' she repeated. 'A very pretty name, my dear.' She was evidently disposed to be friendly to Algernon. 'Much prettier than William, don't you think?'

'Yes,' said William with an expression of sheeplike guilelessness.

Then her gaze descended to an excrescence in William's pocket. It was an apple – the last remaining one of his morning's haul that he'd put in his pocket for refreshment on the way to the Vicarage. Suspicion replaced the lady's friendliness.

'What's that?' she said sharply, pointing to it. William was not for a second at a loss. He drew it out of his pocket and held it out to her.

'I was bringing it back to you,' he said. 'I got him to give it me. It was the only one he had left when he told me about it an' I pled with him —'

'You what?'

'Pled,' said William rather impatiently. 'Don't you know what pleadin' is? Beggin' a person. Askin' 'em. Well, I pled with him to give it me to bring back to you an' to tell you he was sorry an' to ask you not to – to – to come – come troublin' my dear parents about it.'

No words could describe the earnestness of William's voice, the almost imbecile innocence of his regard. The lady's suspicions were entirely lulled. She was more deeply touched than ever.

'I'd like *you* to keep that apple, Algernon,' she said generously, 'but you must promise not to give it to your brother. Will you promise?'

William slipped back the apple into his pocket and duly promised. He promised with quite a clean conscience. He certainly hadn't any intention of giving the apple to Robert. The lady was still looking at him in a friendly fashion.

'I'm afraid that William must be rather a trouble to you, my dear boy,' she said.

'Yes, he is,' said William sadly.

'And I'm sure you do your best to improve him.'

'Yes,' sighed William, 'I'm always at it.'

'Don't despair, my dear boy,' she said, 'I expect

your example will have its effect in the end. You told him how wrong he'd been this morning, I suppose?'

'Oh yes,' said William hastily. 'I told him that all right, I pled with him about it.'

'You must speak to him again about it. You must tell him how *wrong* trespassing is. Tell him that a person who hasn't a clear idea of *meum* and *tuum* comes to no good in the end. And those apples and fishes are *mine*. I paid for them. Surely he knows that stealing's wrong?'

'I'm always telling him,' said William with a sigh, 'pleadin' with him an' such-like.'

'And can't you persuade him to be clean and tidy as you are?' she went on. 'He looked *disgraceful*. I've never seen such a dirty, untidy boy.'

'I'm always pleadin' with him about that too,' said William earnestly. 'I'm always askin' him why he can't be clean and tidy like what I am.'

'Dear boy,' said the lady, laying a hand affectionately on his head, 'I feel that you and I are going to be great friends. My name is Miss Murgatroyd. Together we must try and improve poor William.'

'Yes, an' – an' you – er – won't go troublin' my dear parents?' said William anxiously.

'No, my boy, set your mind at rest. I hope they realize what a dear little protector they have in you.'

William, not knowing what else to do, cleared

his throat and rolled his eyes. Then to his relief she said, 'Well, I must get on now as I have some other calls to pay. Goodbye, Algernon.'

'Goodbye,' said William.

The interview had been enjoyable but rather difficult. For one thing it had been a strain to retain his virtuous and mournful expression throughout it. His face, in fact, ached from his virtuous and mournful expression.

The visit to the vicarage was dull except that the vicar said to one of his guests who ejaculated 'Crumbs!' 'Don't use that vulgar expression, my boy. If you wish to express surprise, say simply "How you do surprise me!" or, if you wish to use stronger language, say "Dear me!" ' – and that somehow or other – no-one quite knew how – a quiet spelling game organized by the vicar became a far from quiet game of Red Indians organized by William, and finally grew so unmanageable that the vicar retired in despair to his study to calm his mind by reading *The Church Times*, and his wife only restored order by distributing pieces of her treacle cake wholesale, and then packing the guests off home. They rollicked homeward down the lanes ejaculating at intervals 'How you do surprise me!' or 'Dear me!' – while the vicar was saying to his wife, 'They are very trying, my dear, but I do think that they gain something of refinement and culture from their little visits here.'

William, on reaching home, went straight to the shed where his aquarium was kept and counted its inhabitants. It still had only one hundred and twenty. There were eighty more to be got. He must pay another visit to Miss Murgatroyd's pond. In any case, it would be rather dull to leave the situation as it was.

The next morning he set off as usual to The Laburnums carrying his fishing paraphernalia. He spent a very happy morning in the orchard and by the pond. He exercised greater caution than before, frequently turning round to make sure that his enemy was not again approaching from the rear. So cautious was he that he saw his enemy approaching as soon as she entered the orchard, and hastily gathered up his paraphernalia and took to his heels without wasting time on any unnecessary courtesies. She did not pursue him, but her words reached him clearly as he fled across the orchard to his hole.

'I shall *certainly* tell your parents this time, William. I only let you off yesterday for your brother's sake. I shall not let you off again.'

William ran down the road without stopping to reply and went straight to the shed where he kept his aquarium, to put in his day's bag and count the whole. He hadn't got as many today as he thought he had. Only twenty. He must have dropped some in his headlong flight. He'd still sixty to get. He must get those tomorrow. He *must* get those tomorrow. William had a bump of determination that would put most ordinary bumps of determination to shame. He'd decided to have two hundred fishes in his aquarium, and it was going to take more than a woman with spectacles and a lot of hair to stop him. He felt quite confident of success. There was still Algernon. The resources of Algernon had surely not yet been exhausted . . .

After lunch, during which William behaved with an exemplariness that aroused his mother's deepest apprehensions, he went up to perform a drastic toilet in secret. His mother was lying down when he crept downstairs in that state of radiant cleanliness and neatness that served as his disguise. His mother would never have believed that William, alone and unaided, could have wrought such a transformation. Even his ears were clean. He wore his best suit. The tabs of his shining boots were tucked in. His knees were pink from scrubbing.

He walked mincingly up to the front door of The Laburnums and rang the bell. He fixed the housemaid who opened the door with a stern and defiant stare.

'Can I speak to Miss Murgatroyd, please?' he said.

The housemaid, who was a stranger to the village, treated him with more politeness than housemaids were in the habit of treating him, and merely said, 'What's your name?'

'W — Algernon Brown,' said William.

'Walgernon, did you say?' said the housemaid surprised.

'No,' said William irritably, 'Algernon.'

He was shown into a drawing-room where Miss Murgatroyd received him affably.

'It's Algernon, isn't it?' she said.

'Yes,' said William, and added with quite convincing anxiety. 'He didn't come this mornin', did he?'

Miss Murgatroyd sighed.

'I'm afraid he did, Algernon,' she said.

'I pled with him not to,' said William sorrowfully. 'I cun't stay with him to stop him comin' 'cause – 'cause an uncle took me up to London. But before I went up I *pled* with him not to come. I told him all you said about trespassin' an' – an' —'

'*Meum* and *tuum*?' supplied Miss Murgatroyd.

'Yes,' said William vaguely. 'An' I asked him how'd he like people comin' into *his* garden an' stealin' *his* apples and fishes. If *he'd* got a garden, I meant.'

'And what did he say to that?'

'He said,' said William unblinkingly, 'he wun't mind at all. He said he'd *like* people to have a few of his apples an' fishes if he'd got any.' He simply couldn't resist saying that.

'But that's very wrong, Algernon,' said Miss Murgatroyd earnestly.

William rolled up his eyes.

'Yes. I told him so,' he said.

'Did he tell you that I was going to tell his parents?'

William cleared his throat and with a superhuman effort deepened his expression of virtue till it bordered again on the imbecile.

'Yes,' he said, 'that's why I came. I came to ask you not to tell them just this once an' I'll do what I can to stop him comin' tomorrow. My – my mother's got a bit of a headache an' so I thought it might worry her hearin' about William takin' your apples an' fishes, but if you'll let him off this once more, I – I'll try 'n' stop him comin' tomorrow. I'll plead with him.'

'But don't you think,' said Miss Murgatroyd earnestly, 'that it would do William *good* to be punished?'

'No,' said William with considerable emphasis, 'I don't think so. I *reely* don't think so. I think it does him far more good to be pled with.'

'Well, I can tell you,' said Miss Murgatroyd with great severity, 'if I'd got him here now I'd box his ears most soundly. Will you have a piece of cake, Algernon dear?'

He signified that he would and she opened a corner cupboard, brought out a rich currant cake and cut him a generous slice. He ate it, making a violent effort to display that restraint and daintiness

219

that he felt would have characterized the obnoxious Algernon. She watched him fondly.

'You certainly are *very* like your twin,' she said at last, but she spoke without any suspicion. 'Which did you say has the longer nose?'

William had forgotten, but he said 'Me' with such an air of conviction that Miss Murgatroyd believed him and said, 'Yes, I see that you have, now you mention it.'

'So – so you won't tell 'em about William?' he said when he had finished.

Miss Murgatroyd considered.

'Well,' she said at last, 'just because your consideration for your parents touches me, Algernon, I won't this once. But you may tell William from me that the very next time I find him trespassing and stealing on my property I'll come *straight* and tell his father. Will you tell him that from me?'

'Yes,' said William anxiously, 'I'll tell him that from you.'

He rose to take his leave. He felt that there was considerable danger in these interviews and that the sooner they were brought to an end the better.

'And what place in London did your uncle take you to, Algernon?' said Miss Murgatroyd.

'The Tower,' said William at random.

'And did you like the beefeaters?'

'It was the Tower I said we went to,' said William, 'not the Zoo.'

Then he went home. His mother greeted him with pleased surprise.

'So you've got ready to go to the garden party with me, dear,' she said; 'how *very* good of you.'

William had forgotten that he was going out to a garden party with her, but he hastily assumed his virtuous expression (he was getting really quite adept at assuming his virtuous expression) and, seeing no escape, prepared to set off.

The garden party was as dull as grown-up garden parties usually are, except that the hostess had a son about William's age who took William to show him the shrubbery. William invented several interesting games to play in the shrubbery and they had quite an enjoyable time there, only emerging on receiving imperative messages from their mothers to come out of it at once. William rejoined his mother, but before she could voice her disapproval of his now dishevelled appearance her harassed frown changed to a smile of social greeting. Her hostess was bringing a new-comer to the neighbourhood to introduce to her. The newcomer was Miss Murgatroyd. She greeted Mrs Brown and then looked uncertainly at William. He wasn't quite dirty enough to be William. On the other hand he wasn't quite clean enough to be Algernon.

'This is – er —?' she began.

'William,' said Mrs Brown.

William met her gaze with an utterly expressionless countenance.

'Your other little boy isn't here, then?' went on Miss Murgatroyd.

'No,' said Mrs Brown, rather surprised to hear the seventeen-year-old Robert referred to as a 'little boy', but assuming that the phrase was meant to be facetious.

'He and I are great friends,' went on Miss Murgatroyd coyly; 'give him my love, will you?' She glanced coldly at William. 'I'm sure you wish that this one would copy him in behaviour and tidiness.'

'Yes,' said Mrs Brown with a sigh, 'I do, indeed.'

Then with a final stern and meaning glance at William, who met it with his blankest stare, she went on in the wake of her hostess to be introduced to someone else.

Mrs Brown gazed after her in bewilderment.

'How funny,' she said. 'Robert's never mentioned meeting her. I must ask him.'

William had heaved a sigh of relief. It had seemed almost incredible that this meeting should have passed off without betraying his double life, but it had. He knew, however, that it could not be sustained much longer. Miss Murgatroyd would be certain to learn sooner or later of the non-existence of Algernon. The time was short. He must finish his aquarium tomorrow and then let events take their course. He'd only got sixty fishes to catch now.

The next morning he tried to elude his enemy by

arriving at an earlier hour than usual. He thought that he had been successful till he was setting off homewards. Then he saw his enemy watching him grimly from an upper window and he knew that all was over. Algernon would be of no avail now. In any case he was getting sick of Algernon. He felt that he'd rather let events take their course than submit himself again to the torturing and degrading process of cleansing and tidying that Algernon's character demanded. And he'd got his fishes. He felt a glow of pride and triumph. He'd got his two hundred fishes. He didn't want ever to go to her silly pond again. And he was sick of her apples. They didn't taste half as nice as they'd tasted at first. He didn't care if he never saw her apples again. Anyway, Ginger was coming home today. He was looking forward to showing Ginger his aquarium.

'What are you going to do this afternoon, dear?' said his mother at lunch.

'I'm going to tea to Ginger's,' said William.

'Well, you mustn't go till I've seen you're tidy,' said Mrs Brown. 'You look dreadful now. Whatever *have* you been doing this morning?'

It was some time before she passed William's appearance as fit for his visit to Ginger's home. Though Ginger's mother saw William daily in his normal state Mrs Brown had a pathetic trust that, if she sent him inordinately cleaned and tidied for all formal visits, Ginger's mother would come to believe that he really was like that. He set off jauntily enough, but at the bend in the road collided with Miss Murgatroyd. He looked round for escape but saw none. So he assumed a blend of his virtuous and defiant expressions and awaited events.

'William came again this morning, Algernon,' said Miss Murgatroyd, 'and I'm on my way now to speak to your parents about him. Nothing you say will make any difference to me. I have finally made up my mind. You must come with me, Algernon, and I will tell them how you have tried to spare their feelings.'

So because there didn't seem to be anything else to do, William went with her.

Mrs Brown was in the drawing-room. She received William's return so soon after setting out with something of bewilderment and the visit of this strange neighbour with even more surprise.

'I've come,' began Miss Murgatroyd without wasting time on preliminaries, 'to complain of your son William.' William assumed his blankest expression and avoided his mother's eyes. 'He has persistently and deliberately trespassed in my grounds, robbed my orchard and fished in my pond. This dear child of yours,' she went on laying her hand affectionately on William's head, 'has done all in his power to protect him and to spare your feelings.' William, looking blanker still, studiously avoided his mother's astounded gaze. 'He

224

begged me not to complain of him to you. He has tried to induce William to stop trespassing in my grounds. He has pleaded with him – pleaded, not pled, Algernon. You are fortunate indeed in having a dear little son like Algernon.'

Mrs Brown's amazement was turning to apprehension.

'Er – just one minute,' she said faintly. Then to her relief she saw her husband's figure pass the window. 'There's my husband. I'll go —' she went hastily from the room to warn her husband that the visitor suffered from delusions and must presumably be humoured.

William, left alone with the visitor, looked desperately about him. The window was the only possible means of escape.

'I – I think I see William in the garden,' he said hoarsely. 'I'll go an' —'

He plunged through the window and disappeared.

His first thought was to carry the aquarium with its two hundred inhabitants out of the reach of paternal vengeance. Ginger had come to meet him and was waiting at the front gate, so together they carried the precious pail to their stronghold, the old barn. Ginger's excitement and admiration knew no bounds.

'It's the finest one I've ever seen,' he said, and added wistfully, 'I bet you had some fun getting it.'

'Oh yes,' said William meaningly, 'I had some fun all right,' and added, 'what sort 'f a holiday 've you had?'

'Rotten,' said Ginger mournfully. 'Everyone cross. *Everyone*. Didn't come across a single person all the time that wasn't cross.'

At this point Douglas joined them. Douglas, too, had just returned from his holiday.

His raptures over William's aquarium were as ardent and genuine as Ginger's. But after about ten minutes, he suddenly remembered something and said to William:

'When I passed your house there was your father and mother and another woman all out in the road looking for you.'

'Did they look mad?' said William with interest.

'Yes, they did, rather,' said Douglas.

'Well, it doesn't matter much,' said William resignedly, 'I've got the fishes away all right, anyway. They can't throw them away now. That's the only thing that really matters. An' I'll give 'em time to get over it a bit before I go home.'

'How did you get 'em all, William?' said Ginger and Douglas as they hung spell-bound over the pail.

William settled down comfortably by his beloved aquarium and chuckled.

'I'll tell you about it,' he said.

This story is by Richmal Crompton.

The Hookywalker Dancers

In the heart of the great city of Hookywalker was the School of Dramatic Art. It was full of all sorts of actors and singers and wonderful clowns, but the most famous of them all was the great dancer, Brighton.

Brighton could leap like an antelope and spin like a top. He was as slender as a needle. In fact, when he danced you almost expected little stitches to follow him across the stage. Every day he did his exercises at the barre to music played on his tape-recorder.

'One and a *plié* and a stretch, two-three, and *port de bras* and back to first!' he counted. He exercised so gracefully that, outside the School of Dramatic Art, pedlars rented ladders so that lovers of the dance could climb up and look through the window at Brighton practising.

Of course, life being what it is, many other dancers were often jealous of him. I'm afraid

227

that most of them ate too much and were rather fat, whereas Brighton had an elegant figure. They pulled his chair away from under him when he sat down, or tried to trip him up in the middle of his dancing, but Brighton was so graceful he simply made falling down look like an exciting new part of the dance, and the people standing on ladders clapped and cheered and banged happily on the windows.

Although he was such a graceful dancer, Brighton was not conceited. He led a simple life. For instance, he didn't own a car, travelling everywhere on roller skates, his tape-recorder clasped to

228

his ear. Not only this, he did voluntary work for the Society for Bringing Happiness to Dumb Beasts. At the weekends he would put on special performances for pets and farm animals. Savage dogs became quiet as lambs after watching Brighton dance, and nervous sheep grew wool thicker than ever before. Farmers from outlying districts would ring up the School of Dramatic Art and ask if they could hire Brighton to dance to their cows, and many a parrot, temporarily off its seed, was brought back to full appetite by seeing Brighton dance the famous solo called *The Noble Savage in the Lonely Wood*.

Brighton had a way of kicking his legs up that suggested deep sorrow, and his *demi-pliés* regularly brought tears to the eyes of the parrots, after which they tucked into their seed quite ravenously.

One day, the director of the School of Dramatic Art called Brighton to his office.

'Brighton,' he said, 'I have an urgent request here from a farmer who needs help with a flock of very nervous sheep. He is in despair!'

'Glad to help!' said Brighton in his graceful fashion. 'What seems to be the trouble?'

'Wolves – that's what the trouble is!' cried the director. 'He lives on the other side of the big forest, and a pack of twenty wolves comes out of the forest early every evening and tries to devour some of his prize merinos. It's disturbing

229

the sheep very badly. They get nervous twitches, and their wool is falling out from shock.'

'I'll set off at once,' Brighton offered. 'I can see it's an urgent case.'

'It's a long way,' the director said, doubtfully. 'It's right on the other side of the forest.'

'That's all right,' said Brighton. 'I have my trusty roller skates, and the road is tarred all the way. I'll take my tape-recorder to keep me company, and I'll get there in next to no time.'

'That's very fast,' the director said in a respectful voice. 'Oh, Brighton, I wish all my dancers were like you! Times are hard for the School of Dramatic Art. A lot of people are staying at home and watching car crashes on television. They don't want art – they want danger, they want battle, murder and sudden death – and it's becoming much harder to run the school at a profit. If all our dancers were as graceful as you there would be no problem at all, but as you know a lot of them are just a whisker on the fat side. They don't do their exercises the way they should.'

Little did he realize that the other dancers were actually listening at the key hole, and when they heard this critical remark they all began to sizzle with jealousy. You could hear them sizzling with it. 'I'll show him who's fat and who isn't,' muttered a very spiteful dancer called Antoine. 'Where are Brighton's skates?'

Brighton's skates were, in fact, in the cloak-room under the peg on which he hung his beret and his great billowing cape. It was but the work of a moment to loosen one or two vital grommets. The skates looked all right, but they were no longer as safe as skates ought to be.

'There,' said Antoine, laughing nastily. 'They'll hold together for a little bit, but once he gets into the forest they'll collapse, and we'll see how he gets on then, all alone with the wind and the wolves – and without wheels.'

The halls of the School of Dramatic Art rang with the jealous laughter of the other dancers as they slunk off in all directions. A minute later Brighton came in, suspecting nothing, put on his beret and his great billowing cape, strapped on his skates, and set off holding his tape-recorder to his ear.

Now, during the day the wolves spent a long time snoozing and licking their paws clean in a clearing on top of the hill. From there they had a good view of the Hookywalker road. They could look out in all directions and even see as far as Hookywalker when the air was clear. It happened that their present king was a great thinker, and something was worrying him deeply.

'I know we're unpopular,' sighed the King of the Wolves, 'but what can I do about it? It's in the nature of things that wolves steal a few sheep here and there. It's part of the great pattern of nature.' Though this seemed reasonable he was frowning and brooding as he spoke. 'Sometimes – I don't know – I feel there must be more to life than just ravening around grabbing the odd sheep and howling at the moon.'

'Look!' cried the wolf who was on look-out duty. 'Someone is coming down the great road from the city.'

'How fast he's going!' said another wolf. 'And whatever is it he is holding to his ear?'

'Perhaps he has earache,' suggested a female wolf in compassionate tones. None of the wolves had ever seen a tape-recorder before.

'Now then, no feeling sorry for him,' said the King of the Wolves. 'You all know the drill. We get down to the edge of the road, and at the first chance we tear him to pieces. That's all part of the great pattern of nature I was mentioning a moment ago.'

'That'll take his mind off his earache,' said one of the wolves with a fierce, sarcastic snarl.

As the sun set majestically in the west, Brighton, his cloak billowing round him like a private storm cloud, reached the great forest. It was like entering another world, for a mysterious twilight reigned under the wide branches, a twilight without moon

232

or stars. Tall, sombre pines looked down as if they feared the worst. But Brighton skated on, humming to himself. He was listening to the music of *The Noble Savage* and was waiting for one of the parts he liked best. Indeed, so busy was he humming and counting the beats that he did not notice a sudden wobble in his wheels. However, a moment after the wobble, his skates gave a terrible screech and he was pitched into the pine needles by the side of the road.

'Horrakapotchkin!' cried Brighton. 'My poor skates!' (It was typical of this dancer that his first thought was for others.) However, his second thought was of the forest and the wolves that might be lurking there. It occurred to him that they might be tired of merino sheep, and would fancy a change of diet.

'Quick thought! Quick feet!' he said, quoting an old dancing proverb. He rushed around collecting a pile of firewood and pine cones, and then lit a good-sized fire there on the roadside. It was just as well he did, because when he looked up he saw the forest was alight with fiery red eyes. The wolves had arrived. They stole out of the forest and sat down on the edge of the fire light, staring at him very hard, all licking their lips in a meaningful way.

Brighton did not panic. Quietly, he rewound his tape-recorder to the very beginning, and then stood up coolly and began to do his exercises. A lesser dancer might have started off dancing straight away, but Brighton knew the greatest challenge of his life was ahead of him. He preferred to take things slowly and warm up properly in case he needed to do a few tricky steps before the night was out.

The wolves looked at each other uneasily. The king hesitated. There was something so tuneful about the music and so graceful about Brighton's dancing that he would have liked to watch it for a bit longer, but he knew he was part of nature's great plan, and must help his pack to tear Brighton to pieces. So he gave the order. 'Charge!'

As one wolf the wolves ran towards Brighton, snarling and growling, but to their astonishment Brighton did not run away. No! He actually ran towards them and then, leaped up in the air – up, up and right over them – his cloak streaming out behind him. It had the words *Hookywalker School of Dramatic Art* painted on it. The wolves were going so fast that they could not stop themselves until they were well down the road. Brighton, meanwhile, landed with a heroic gesture, wheeled around, and then went on with his exercises, watching the wolves narrowly.

Once again, the wolves charged, and once again Brighton leaped. This time he jumped even higher, and the wolves couldn't help gasping in admiration, much as they hated missing out on any prey.

'Right!' cried the King of the Wolves. 'Let's run round him in ever-decreasing circles.' (This was an old wolf trick.) 'He'll soon be too giddy to jump.' However, being a wolf and not used to classical ballet, the king didn't realize that a good dancer can spin on his toes without getting in the least bit giddy. Brighton spun until he was a mere blur and actually rose several inches in the air with the power of his rotation. It was the wolves who became giddy first; they stumbled over one another, ending up in a heap, with their red eyes all crossed. Finally, they struggled up with their tongues hanging out but they had to wait for their eyes to get uncrossed again.

Seeing they were disabled for the moment by the wonder of his dancing, Brighton now gave up mere jumps and spins and began demonstrating his astonishing technique. Used as he was to dancing for animals, there was still a real challenge about touching the hearts of wolves. Besides, he knew he couldn't go on twirling and leaping high in the air all night. His very life depended on the quality of his dancing. He began with the first solo from *The Noble Savage*. Never in all his life, even at the School of Dramatic Art, had he been more graceful. First, he danced the loneliness of the Noble Savage, and the wolves (though they always travelled in a pack, and were never ever lonely) were so stirred that several of them pointed their noses into the air and howled in exact time to the music. It was most remarkable. Brighton now turned towards the wolves and began to express through dance his pleasure at seeing them. He made it very convincing. Some of the wolves began to wag their tails.

'He's really got something!' said the King of the Wolves. 'This is high-class stuff.' Of course, he said it in wolf language, but Brighton was good at reading the signs and became more poetic than ever before.

'Let me see,' said the King of the Wolves, fascinated. 'With a bit of practice I could manage an act like this myself. I always knew there was more to life than mere ravening. Come on! Let's give it a go!' The wolves began to point their paws and copy whatever movements Brighton made.

Seeing what they were about, Brighton began to encourage them by doing a very simple step and shouting instructions.

'You put your left paw in, you put your left paw out . . .'

Of course, the wolves could not understand the words, but Brighton was very clever at mime and they caught on to the idea of things, dancing with great enthusiasm. Naturally, they were not as graceful as Brighton, but then they had not practised for years as he had. Brighton could not help but be proud of them as they began a slow progress down the road back to the city, away from

236

the forest and the sheep on the other side. The moon
rose higher in the sky, and still Brighton danced,
and the entranced wolves followed him pointing
their paws. It was very late at night when they
entered the city once more. People going home
from the cinema stared and shouted, and pointed
(fingers not toes). A lot of them joined in, either
dancing or making music on musical instruments
– banjos, trombones, combs – or anything that
happened to be lying around.

In the School of Dramatic Art, wicked Antoine
was just about to dance the very part Brighton usually danced when the sound of the procession made

him hesitate. The audience, full of curiosity, left the theatre. Outside was Brighton, swaying with weariness but still dancing, followed by twenty wolves, all dancing most beautifully by now, all in time and all very pleased with themselves, though, it must be admitted, all very hungry.

'Oh,' cried the director of the School of Dramatic Art, rushing out to kiss Brighton on both cheeks. 'What talent! What style! This will save the School of Dramatic Art from extinction.'

'Send out for a supply of sausages,' panted Brighton, 'and write into the wolves' contracts that they will have not only sausages of the best quality, but that their names will appear in lights on top of the theatre. After all, if they are dancing here every night, they won't be able to chase and worry sheep, will they?'

After this, there was peace for a long time, both in the city and out on the farms (where the sheep grew very fat and woolly). The School of Dramatic Art did wonderfully well. People came from miles around to see Brighton and his dancing wolves, and, of course – just as he had predicted – after dancing until late at night, the wolves were too weary to go out ravening sheep. Everyone was delighted (except for the jealous dancers who just sulked and sizzled). Antoine, in particular, had such bad attacks of jealousy that it ruined his digestion and made his stomach rumble loudly, which forced him to abandon ballet altogether. However, Brighton, the wolves, the farmers, the director, and many other people, lived happily ever after in Hookywalker, that great city which people sometimes see looming out of the mist on the fringe of many fairy stories.

This story is by Margaret Mahy.

A SELECTED LIST OF TITLES
AVAILABLE FROM CORGI BOOKS

☐	0 552 527181	**A POCKETFUL OF STORIES FOR FIVE YEAR OLDS**	*Pat Thomson*	£2.99
☐	0 552 527572	**A BUCKETFUL OF STORIES FOR SIX YEAR OLDS**	*Pat Thomson*	£2.99
☐	0 552 527297	**A BASKET OF STORIES FOR SEVEN YEAR OLDS**	*Pat Thomson*	£2.99
☐	0 552 527300	**A SACKFUL OF STORIES FOR EIGHT YEAR OLDS**	*Pat Thomson*	£2.99
☐	0 552 527580	**A CHEST OF STORIES FOR NINE YEAR OLDS**	*Pat Thomson*	£2.99

All Corgi Books are available at your bookshop or newsagent, or can be ordered from the following address:
Transworld Publishers Ltd,
Cash Sales Department,
PO Box 11, Falmouth, Cornwall TR10 9EN

Please send a cheque or postal order (no currency) and allow £1.00 for postage and packing for one book, an additional 50p for a second book, and an additional 30p for each subsequent book ordered to a maximum charge of £3.00 if ordering seven or more books.

Overseas customers, including Eire, please allow £2.00 for postage and packing for the first book, an additional £1.00 for a second book, and an additional 50p for each subsequent title ordered.

NAME (Block Letters) ....

ADDRESS ....

....

A SACKFUL OF STORIES FOR EIGHT YEAR OLDS
Collected by PAT THOMSON
Illustrated by Paddy Mounter

Delve into this sack of stories and you will find . . . a Martian wearing Granny's jumper, that well-known comic fairy-tale pair Handsel and Gristle, a unicorn, a leprechaun, a princess who is a pig, and many other strange and exciting characters. You won't want to stop reading until you get right to the bottom of the sack!

'There are thirteen stories to a sackful and each and every one is a tried-and-tested cracker'
The Sunday Telegraph

'Will be enjoyed by children of all ages'
The Times Educational Supplement

'Will stimulate even the most reluctant reader'
Junior Education

Read Alone or Read Aloud

0 552 527300

A BASKET OF STORIES FOR SEVEN YEAR OLDS
Collected by PAT THOMSON
Illustrated by Rachel Birkett

Climb into this basket of stories and you will find
. . . Charlie and his puppy, a wolf that tells riddles, a
witch, a smelly giant, and many other strange and
exciting people and animals. You won't want to stop
reading until you get right to the bottom of the
basket!

'Jam-packed with goodies' *The Sunday Telegraph*

'Will be enjoyed by children of all ages'
The Times Educational Supplement

'Will stimulate even the most reluctant reader'
Junior Education

Read Alone or Read Aloud

0 552 527297

A BUCKETFUL OF STORIES FOR
SIX YEAR OLDS
Collected by PAT THOMSON
Illustrated by Mark Southgate

Dip into this bucketful of stories and you will find
. . . a ghost who lives in a cupboard, a dog that saves
a ship, a king who can turn things into gold, a dwarf
who becomes a cat, and many other strange and exciting people and animals. You won't want to stop
reading until you get right to the bottom of the buc-
ket!

'Well suited to the stated age group . . . the mixture
seems guaranteed to please' *The Times Educational
Supplement*

Read Alone or Read Aloud

0 552 527572